"I'"

Abby said the words through the closed door. He didn't say anything else, and she hoped he'd gone away.

"Are you sure?" He hadn't.

She faked a noisy yawn. "Yeah. Thanks, but I'm tired."

Holding her breath, she waited for him to take the hint. She couldn't face him yet. If she wasn't careful, she might tell him the truth.

At last he walked away. "Good night." From the sound of his voice, he'd already taken several steps down the hall.

She breathed again, air leaving her lungs in a whoosh that made her head spin faster. Panting for more oxygen, she thought she might be sick. Twenty-nine years old, and she wanted Thomas so much she hadn't remembered to keep herself safe.

And what about him? He didn't deserve a lifetime obligation. He'd come to her for help, not fatherhood.

Dear Reader,

Her Little Secret is the fourth novel in the WOMEN IN BLUE series—six books about women who met and befriended each other during their police academy training.

Patrolman Abby Carlton and soldier Thomas Riley have history, but her skills as a member of Houston PD's Crisis Intervention Team lead him to trust her with his secrets when a battlefield skirmish goes wrong. After a night of passion, Abby has a secret she's keeping from Thomas. Together they face a stalker and their own doubts about each other and the careers that have kept them apart. Just in time, they learn that two people lucky enough to find true love share all their secrets.

I'd love to hear what you think. You can reach me at anna@annaadams.net. And don't forget to look for the other WOMEN IN BLUE, by Kay David, Linda Style, Sherry Lewis, Roz Denny Fox and K.N. Casper. You won't want to miss any of these complicated women or their touching stories.

Best wishes,

Anna

Her Little Secret

Anna Adams

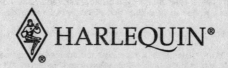

HARLEQUIN®

TORONTO • NEW YORK • LONDON
AMSTERDAM • PARIS • SYDNEY • HAMBURG
STOCKHOLM • ATHENS • TOKYO • MILAN • MADRID
PRAGUE • WARSAW • BUDAPEST • AUCKLAND

ISBN 0-373-71248-0

HER LITTLE SECRET

Copyright © 2005 by Anna Adams.

www.eHarlequin.com

Printed in U.S.A.

To Karen Whiddon. I'm always grateful for your
careful reading, and I count on your critique,
but it's your friendship I'll always treasure most.

To my fellow WOMEN IN BLUE authors, Kay David,
Sherry Lewis, Linda Style, Roz Denny Fox and K.N. Casper.
I always wondered what it would be like to work in a group,
bounce ideas, plot through story problems with other
authors. You made the work fun, the process even more
creative. I'm proud to be part of this group, proud of
our work, but a little sad to see the process
come to an end. Heartfelt thanks to all of you!

CHAPTER ONE

OLD HABITS DIED HARD.

Thomas Riley parked his rental car a block from Abby Carlton's house. Ambling—no more dangerous than a guy out for a walk—he reconnoitered the area. A middle-class neighborhood, not shabby, not chic.

Cars whizzed past. Tree branches hung too low over the cracked sidewalks. Children had tossed their bikes and basketballs and Big Wheels into heaps on their front yards. One family's oversize garbage cans wore a coat of rain and mud from a recent, obviously violent storm.

Thomas tracked the house numbers without looking directly at them. As he neared Abby's home, a cracked, off-key voice cut the air. Despite being totally tone-deaf, Abby Carlton sang whenever she felt like it.

Only a glass storm door stood between the house and the rest of the world. Even the windows on the ground floor were open, just begging someone to rip off a screen and climb into the small green house.

Abby increased her volume, reaching a powerful point in a song Thomas had never heard. He spent too little time in the States to recognize the top forty.

Her singing nearly drove him back to his car. Not because she stank, though she'd be wise to keep her job as a cop, but Thomas hated to ruin her good mood. He'd come to beg for help from the one woman on earth who might hate him too much to care.

He twisted his neck. Children's voices, birdsong, racing car engines all faded, leaving only Abby's tuneless joy and the pain that rode up his spine to knot at the back of his head.

She drew nearer. He'd thought he was ready to see her, but he was wrong. Thomas stared at her through the closest window.

Six years after she'd left she remained unfinished business. But no one else could help him.

She stopped on "heav—" and pressed her face to the screen. Her nose flattened. Small holes in the mesh speckled her forehead.

"Thomas?" She said his name as if it was hard to pronounce and then leaned back. "Thomas Riley?" Inside the house, something clattered onto a wooden floor. "Thomas." She backed away, only a shadow in the window.

He checked over one shoulder and then the other, aware of her neighbors, none of whom bothered with him. Seconds dragged.

She didn't appear in the doorway. The windows

stayed blank. Thomas swore. Abby had never hidden from anything, but now she seemed to be hiding from him.

He marched to the porch. Just as he pointed his index finger at the lighted white button to ring the bell, she walked into the hall.

"You're about six years late."

She cared—as in worried about people—more than anyone he'd ever known, but she must still be pissed. He wanted to tell her he was a dedicated soldier who'd only thrown away their engagement because he'd believed in his job. Even in his head that sounded pompous and lame.

"You left me." It was a defensive reflex, but for six years, he'd thought he was right not to follow her to Houston.

"You were long gone before I packed my things." Abby lifted both hands to her temples, freeing almost-black strands of hair from a short ponytail. "Let's not launch into the same old argument. We couldn't fix anything then, and nothing's changed. You have more important problems."

Disdain frosted her voice, and he narrowed his eyes. He had more problems than she could know. He couldn't control his feelings anymore. He was supposed to be a dispassionate leader, the man his team counted on to make the right decision. Instead, he'd let guilt and rage fog his judgment, and his men had been killed, along with a civilian female and her three children.

"I'm in trouble." Sand and blood and the dead faces of his innocent victims filled his mind.

Abby looked at him and then looked again, seeing too much. Her sympathy hurt a lot more than contempt.

She reached for the door handle, her mouth tight. "What do you need?"

To slay a few demons and persuade her he was worth extra trouble. "I never chose to leave you. I'm in the Army. I have to report when they tell me."

Abby didn't answer, but she opened the door. She glanced down, plainly uncomfortable with her sweats' dirty knees and a snug T-shirt that barely skimmed her navel.

She lived in a world that no longer existed for him, where normal people cared what they looked like. Where they left jobs at five o'clock and never had to deal with the anguish they'd caused.

Normal people didn't kill. Moisture filmed his hands. He wasn't normal anymore, but he couldn't lead his men if he dreaded killing to save them.

Abby wrapped her arms around herself. "Your eyes make me cold."

"It's cold on this side of them, too."

She opened her mouth a little, the way she did when she was surprised. Why? He'd always been honest with her.

"Come inside and tell me what you need."

He couldn't move. He should thank her, but he didn't know how. He hesitated on the threshold. She'd never look at him the same way. He had to expose his secrets, and even he wasn't sure he was much of a man.

His footsteps on Abby Carlton's creaking floor startled him.

"What's wrong with you, Thomas?" Abby, the cop, looked him over, interrogating him without words. "You're different. Not your looks." She saw past his long hair and unshaven face. "You were never supposed to look like a regular soldier." Then she zeroed in on his face. "Someone's beaten the arrogance out of you."

"I did it myself." But he wasn't out of the battle yet. "I can't get it back on my own, and I need it to do my job. I don't believe in myself anymore, and I can't lead my men unless I do."

ABBY HAD NO ANSWER. Stunned to find him on her doorstep, astounded to discover he had a flaw, much less that he could admit it, she felt as if she was facing a stranger.

Yet, his eyes. They were empty and broken—reminding her of her mother's during an episode of the bipolar disease that had haunted Abby's family for years.

Six years ago, Thomas had attracted her with his

strength. Certain of himself, of his decisions, he'd never looked back, hardly ever worried about the future, preferring to live entirely in the here and now, where he was in control.

That had appealed to Abby, who'd never known what would trigger one of her mother's depressive phases. She'd been her mother's caretaker, her father's friend, her own parent. She'd loved Thomas partly because he hadn't needed her, until she'd realized he needed his job more.

"What's wrong with you?" she asked.

"I need help."

"I need specifics." She pushed the door shut, careful not to touch him. He still had the ascetic face and innocent blue eyes of a saint. He'd never looked like the kind of man who'd kill to save a secret or risk his own life to snatch an operative who could help his government. Dark smudges and wary lines on his face made Abby want to do something—comfort him—promise that whatever was wrong wouldn't hurt him forever.

Instead she turned the dead bolt and reminded herself she didn't have to make anything better for Thomas. She owed him no more concern than he'd given her. But he'd held her heart, and she couldn't turn her back on him.

Setting the locks was the sort of comfort he'd appreciate. During the year they'd lived together he'd trained her to take extra precautions because his job put him in contact with people who might want him dead.

"You have to explain," she said.

"I'll try." He pressed two fingers of each hand onto his eyes as if they hurt. Longish, wavy brown hair shielded his face. Finally, he looked at her, hiding nothing. "I didn't know where else to go."

Thomas had never asked for so much as a hot meal—even after he'd traveled twenty-four hours, returning from one of his "trips."

"How bad is it?"

"I'm here," he said, and no emotion showed on his face. It was all in his voice. Bleak, desperate. So unlike the Thomas she'd had to leave. "I can't sleep. I can't think about who I am or what I'm supposed to do when I go back to North Carolina."

"Can I call someone for you?"

"Who?"

"I don't know. Why come to me? I can't be the best friend you have."

"I remembered your mom's problems. You took care of her when your father had to work. And I know you're on Houston PD's Crisis Intervention Team."

"How do you know all that?" She hadn't looked over her shoulder often enough in the past few years. Apparently he'd been behind her.

"You didn't even leave me a note. And since the best way to get to me was to hurt you, I had to make sure you were all right."

"You didn't have to keep making sure."

"I shouldn't have." A hint of his old arrogance came and went. "But I did, and when I realized I couldn't go back to work yet, I'd hoped maybe you'd forget the past." He looked away as if even he knew he'd asked too much. "And you could talk to me until I understand what's wrong."

"You didn't think this through. I don't have enough training."

He shook his head, ignoring what she'd said. Then he glanced through the doorway on the left, to her living room, where she'd pushed back all the furniture. "I've come at a bad time? Do you have company? What's going on?"

"I was waxing the floors." She tugged down her shirt. "And I look as if I've been dusting with my own clothes." Back to the real point. "You remember we haven't seen each other in six years and we parted on bad terms?"

"None of that matters."

His firm voice was a knife sliding into her skin, a quick cut that stung more with each passing second. "It does to me. I left because I kept expecting some colonel to drive up and tell me you'd died. I loved you, but you loved your job. You didn't mind the idea of dying. Even when you were home, I couldn't seem to get your attention, and finally, the time we spent together wasn't worth the risk of that visit."

"Wasn't worth it?" An unfamiliar edge entered his voice. Thomas always controlled his reactions. She'd never managed to annoy him. He'd only let her feel how much he wanted her in bed, and his desire had begun to make her sad when she'd understood she'd never see it outside that room.

"You didn't try to find me." Why had she mattered so little?

"You couldn't handle my life, and I can't change it. That's why I'm *begging* for help now. I'm a soldier who can't lead his men. I'm a killer who dreads killing, and I'm worried I'll harm my own team next time I'm called on to make a decision."

"Meaning?"

"We were supposed to snatch a cleric. His guards strapped a bomb to a woman's chest and pushed her and her children in front of the guy we wanted. I couldn't tell if she was the enemy, and I hesitated."

Rage threaded his voice, the calm fury of a soldier who'd never made a mistake because he'd done his work without passion, acting only with the force each task required. That much, Abby had known about Thomas. His men had told her.

He rubbed his shoulder, but then flinched, and Abby noticed a lump beneath his shirt.

"Are you hurt?" Fighting trained instincts, she flexed her fingers, itching to check his wounds. In her job, she often had to evaluate the needs of people who lived on the street and then send them where they could get help they needed.

Thomas dropped his hands to his sides and put up the usual barrier between them. "I'm fine, physically, but that woman, her children, the cleric and three of my own men died. Because I hesitated a second."

His story sent her back in time. "I got in trouble because I didn't wait long enough."

"What?"

Thinking about it still bothered her so much she was almost surprised to find Thomas in front of her. "It was my first week on patrol. A guy panicked in a Laundromat when his load of whites never finished. He was sick." She hated remembering. "He didn't understand the machine was broken, and he started throwing baskets and detergent boxes. When he saw my partner and me, he grabbed a girl and barricaded himself in a corner with a hanger. He only let the girl go to take a stab at my partner." Her mouth dried, but when she looked at Thomas his compassion made her go on. "A more experienced officer might have talked him down. I pleaded with him, but he went crazy. I thought I had to shoot."

"Did you?"

She hardly recognized Thomas's strangled tone, filled with all the fear and dread she'd felt that morning. "I still don't know."

"Did he die?"

She shook her head. "I did CPR until the EMTs came. And then I went back to work and applied for the CIT." She left out the part where she'd cried all over the man's bloody chest and prayed he wouldn't die as the words *I have to quit* had repeated in her head. She and Thomas had made a strange new relationship in these few minutes, but he didn't need to know how well she understood his problem. "Won't the Army help you?"

"They say I'm ready to go back." He rubbed his shoulder again. "I want to, but I have to know I won't get anyone else killed."

"Haven't you done enough?" The truth slipped out. She might not love him anymore, but she didn't want him dead.

He turned back into the hall. He was reaching for the door, as if her question meant she'd already made up her mind, and he couldn't count on her to help. She grabbed his arm and felt a bandage on his wrist. His muscles flexed as he grimaced, and she let go.

"Don't leave." Sudden movement caught her eye. Thomas, seeing it, turned, his fists clenched to attack. She stepped in front of him, holding him back as the orange tabby she'd rescued from the pound sauntered out of the kitchen. "It's only Herb," she said.

Fifteen pounds of liberated contentment—as long as he ruled the roost. Her friend in animal control had told her they couldn't find a place for such a big guy. The cute little kitties robbed him of prospective homes. He'd been surly and doubtful when she'd first lured him into her life with kitty treats.

"It's probably snack time."

The cat sat and began to study their guest, and Abby felt Thomas breathing behind her.

They both stared at Herb, who yawned and turned back toward the kitchen with a switch of his tail as if to suggest Abby do her duty by his food dish.

"You can't resist a stray."

She felt the heat of a blush. "You're not a stray, Thomas. I still don't get why you came to me, but I'd like to help. I just don't know how I can with only forty hours of training in de-escalating a crisis. I decide where to send people who need help."

"Try to do more for me." He didn't add *please,* but she heard it in his voice. "If I talk to a therapist in North Carolina or anyone from the government, my Army career is over."

"Would that be so bad? I hated your job."

He lifted his head in half a nod. "But I have to do it—right."

She rolled her hands into the hem of her shirt, too tempted to make sure he was safe from now on. "You need more than I can give, and I still don't want you to be hurt."

He tried to speak, but his throat must have tightened. He cleared it. "Help me, Abby."

"Even if I could, I'm too close to you." The right

person was obvious, though. Liam, her ex, was a psychologist she'd met in the CIT training program. After their divorce, they'd remained friends. He knew how to distance himself from personal feelings, and he believed in ethics. "You should try Liam Webster."

"Your ex-husband?" He headed toward the door again. "Not a chance."

"What *don't* you know about me?" She used her cop voice. He only looked at her.

"Liam keeps secrets, and he's a smart guy."

Looking toward the door—escape—he hesitated. "How do I trust someone you married, Abby?"

She didn't want to answer. She'd met Liam two years after she'd left Thomas, but it hadn't been long enough.

"He's my friend now and you shouldn't care what he was to me."

He clenched his hand around the doorknob. "I do."

She rubbed at a smudge of dirt on her palm to avoid meeting his too-serious, too-open eyes. "I don't know who else to suggest."

"Call one of the other psychologists who trained you."

"I don't know anyone else as well as Liam."

"I can't talk to the man who took my place."

"You know it's possible to be too honest?"

He was stiff, yet vulnerable, pretending to be

strong. He took Abby's breath away. He'd never had to pretend before. Strength had been like his brown hair or blue eyes—part of him.

"I didn't want to lose you," he said. "I couldn't promise marriage and babies, but I tried to be honest."

"Dancing around the truth isn't the same as being faithful to it." She crossed the living room to close a window. "I left my parents behind. I quit my job for you. Imagine how happy the review boards at the academy were to take me back after I quit to follow my boyfriend. I was a useful example for every man who doesn't want women on the force."

"You followed the man you loved. We were committed to each other."

"I committed. You didn't." For the first time since she'd seen him on her walkway, she lost her temper. "After I came back, I had to earn my friends' faith. They couldn't be associated with an unreliable flake. I hurt my parents. They thought I'd run away." She lowered her head, reluctant to admit the most painful part of her past, too far gone in her rant to stop. "I lost you."

He finally let his hand slide off the doorknob. "If I'd known you were leaving, I wouldn't have let you go."

"I don't believe you." She should drop it. Their past meant nothing. He wanted help with a problem that didn't affect her. "Forget it." She squared her shoulders and brought their conversation back to the present. "I don't know anyone except Liam well enough to guarantee your secrets."

"I'm only asking for normal patient confidentiality."

"If the FBI questions Liam, he won't give you up. I can't vouch for anyone else."

"Let me think."

"About what?" But maybe she was the one who should think.

"Are you trying not to get involved again, Abby?"

Behind closed eyelids, she saw the man she'd shot lying on the ground beneath her blood-splashed hands. Her own mother, slumped in a chair, her hair stringy, her eyes empty. Abby took a deep breath and blew it through her lips. She thought of Janie, a homeless woman who often came to her in search of a shelter bed. Even Herb—how could she help a cat, but turn Thomas away?

"I do know someone I could ask." Risa Taylor, who'd been falsely suspected of shooting her partner. The department had been wrong about her, but they still would have made her see a doctor. If her therapist had helped at all, maybe Thomas would find relief there, too.

And Risa was the one friend who'd immediately welcomed Abby back from North Carolina. She'd understood circumstances beyond a woman's control.

"Who do you know? Call him."

"Her. Risa." Abby studied the mantel clock. "It's 6:18. She'll be on her shift already, and I don't want to call her at work about this."

"She's one of those women I met—the ones who went to the academy with you?"

"Yeah."

"And she didn't hold me against you?"

"None of them did, but Crista and Mei were so focused on their careers they couldn't understand why I gave up mine. Lucy and Catherine don't say much, but Risa understood how I felt." As he clenched his fists in his pockets, she turned toward the door. "Where are your bags?"

"What?"

"Oh." According to her practice of going the last inappropriate mile, she'd assumed he'd stay with her.

"You'd let me stay? I didn't want to go to a hotel—too hard to control the situation—but I thought you wouldn't go for it."

She couldn't ignore his pale face or his effort to keep his shoulders soldier-straight.

Herb trotted out of the kitchen again, apparently tired of waiting for the hand that fed him. He'd have to wait a little while longer. If she backed off now, she might change her mind. "Where are your things?" Herb, curious about their visitor, sniffed at Thomas's ankles.

Thomas moved his leg away from the cat. "I left

my bag in my car. I wasn't sure you'd even open the door."

"Well, I'm on the job now." And now was the time to try seeing him as any other wounded victim. "You need to rest." She led him into the living room, but Herb startled her, trotting at Thomas's heels. When Thomas stopped, Herb sat at his side.

"I don't need to rest."

"Trust me. You look like you're about to pass out." Abby put dish towels under the sofa's wooden feet and then leaned into the nearest arm. "I'll get this back in place, and then you can lie down."

Thomas reached for the other side of the couch.

"Don't." She dragged her end back, and Herb fled, his paws thudding, his belly wobbling from side to side.

Thomas watched his escape. "He could lose a few ounces." He reached for the sofa again, but she jerked it away. "What are you doing, Abby?"

"I don't want you to tear any sutures."

"I'm fine physically. Don't treat me like an invalid."

Why argue? If he fainted on the sidewalk, she'd just drag him back to the house. "Where's your car? Let's get your stuff."

"I have a rental down the street. Let me help you lock the windows, and we'll go."

"Fair enough." It had to be, since he wasn't about to give in. She closed the second window and he went to the last one.

"Are they open all over the house?"

"Only on this side. I may not be as careful as you, but I don't take security for granted." And the neighborhood she could afford on a patrol officer's salary wasn't unquestionably safe. She grabbed her jacket off the banister in the hall and then opened the front door. "Ready?"

Nodding, he waited on the porch while she locked up, but when she turned, he was already on the move. As he went down the walk, Abby jumped down her three porch steps. Five-seven, to Thomas's six-three, she hurried to match his stride.

She ignored her neighbors' curious gazes. Even the kids, used to seeing her on neighborhood watch, stopped to watch Thomas.

He stopped at a blue sedan that resembled maybe a million others exactly like it. He opened the passenger door for her. Abby got in, and he went around to drive. He parked across from her place.

"Will anyone mind?" he asked.

"See any two-car garages? We don't have room to be territorial."

He popped the trunk and they met in the back, where he lifted his single duffel from the otherwise empty stretch of carpet.

Abby shut the trunk. "You have faith in a quick cure."

"You weren't always this sarcastic," he said.

She tried to read his expression, but he wouldn't look at her. "I was twenty-one when I knew you. I've changed in my formative years." Since then she'd seen men like him, with no one to turn to. She'd seen her own mother through a suicide attempt that still made her break into a sweat when sirens woke her in the night.

Guilt in his sudden glance made her uncomfortable. "Not because of you." Abby pulled keys out of her pocket and ran ahead to pluck the newspaper and mail out of the box bolted to one of the porch stanchions. She opened the front door. "Are you hungry?"

"I don't like imposing."

"I'll let you know if you are." Inside, she shrugged out of her jacket and flung it back over the banister. "Do you need bandages?"

He looked as reluctant to sample her first-aid kit as the contents of her fridge. "Maybe after we eat."

"Then I'll wash up and cook." She started climbing the stairs, but paused to look back, her hand on the rail. "You want to see your room?"

His progress was stiffer than hers. She tried to slow down without letting him see she had.

"You'll have to use the hall bath." Thank goodness for the privacy of the tiny bath attached to her own room. For months after she'd left North Carolina, she'd missed the intimacy of sharing with Thomas. They'd shared so little else.

"I'm grateful for whatever you have."

His humble response confused her. "I hardly know you, Thomas. You're more human." Which he obviously saw as a problem. "I never expected to see you again."

"You're kind, Abby. I had no right to come. I didn't call first because I wasn't sure I'd go through with asking you."

Unsettled, she opened his bedroom door and switched on the light. The bed was made, but the air smelled stale.

"I should open this more often."

"It's great. Thanks." Standing on the threshold, he pointed his bag toward the bathroom. "Do I have time for a shower?"

Abby nodded. "The towels and linen are in the closet beside the tub." At a sudden memory of Thomas with water cascading down his chest and across her face, she moved toward the door. Any compassionate soul would forgive her hasty retreat. "The first-aid kit's in there, too. Do you need help?"

From his reluctance, he did, but he didn't want her. Fine. She'd rather not see his wounds.

"I have a shrapnel cut on my back that hasn't healed yet."

Her stomach flip-flopped. She'd been better off not knowing. "Why'd they let you leave the hospital?"

"What more could they do?" His bleakness

scared her. "Besides, I had to get help they wouldn't give."

Anger swept her, a Pavlovian response to his sense of duty. She covered her mouth with her fingertips to keep from speaking. She had no right to care that he craved danger, that his uniform and his men meant more to him than himself.

But old habits died hard.

CHAPTER TWO

"MAYBE YOU COULD HELP ME after I shower," Thomas said.

She glanced up to see if pigs had suddenly taken flight around her ceiling. She'd never imagined him willingly asking anyone for help. The change in him startled her, but she pretended everything was just like always. "Good idea. Make yourself at home. I'll wash off the dust and see what's to cook."

Abby sped through a shower, but the water was still running in Thomas's room when she went to the kitchen. She started spaghetti sauce. It wouldn't have time to simmer the way he liked, but he could use a plate of his favorite food.

He came down in jeans, T-shirt and sweater, looking damp, smelling of her floral guest soap. "Point me at the right cupboards, and I'll set the table."

"That one, nearest the sink." Out of the corner of her eye, she watched him set out plates and silverware while she made a salad. It felt like playing house. She pictured sand and heat and people lying in wait around unfamiliar corners, armed to kill.

Playing house had to be a relief for him. "Why don't you get the wineglasses? They're in the dining room."

"You still have your grandmother's sideboard?" He didn't wait for her answer. Abby sagged against the counter, breathing deep only because he wasn't there to hog all the oxygen. He'd loved that sideboard. His own parents had left him nothing of their family's past. Maybe he couldn't face babies and forever, but he'd envied her tangible link with her history.

Abby served as Thomas filled two glasses with ice water and poured the wine. They sat at the same time, their store of small talk exhausted. Thomas polished off two helpings of spaghetti, along with his salad and an impressive share of garlic bread.

"At least you're able to eat." Maybe his appetite meant he was healing. "I wish I could offer dessert."

His grin brought back difficult memories of hurried dinners and early nights in the bed that had overwhelmed her all the nights she'd slept in it alone.

"Your cooking's a lot better," he said. She felt herself blushing. Thomas looked away. He sipped his wine, and the light glinted through facets in the goblet. "I didn't realize I was so hungry."

"Walter Reed's kitchen isn't up to your standards?"

"Food wasn't on my mind."

His war-bitten body and face revealed the details. He'd been trying not to die.

"I'll call Risa in the morning."

"Thanks." He emptied his glass and pushed it until he could only touch it with the tips of his fingers. "Seriously, Abby. Thanks. Maybe you should have turned me out on my ear."

This new Thomas, minus the assumption that the world spun to his pleasure, softened her heart. She should help him—yes. Get involved again—no. And no and no once more. She'd taken years to recover from the knowledge he'd never be able to love her the way she'd needed. She'd married another man on the rebound. No woman's life could afford that kind of trauma twice. "I do the same for strangers every day."

He took the hint. They weren't getting close enough to hurt each other this time. That blank look returned to his eyes. "You don't offer strangers your guest room?"

Janie, her homeless friend, would have slept on the street a few nights if Abby hadn't possessed an extra bed. Janie got to her because her symptoms were so similar to Abby's mom's.

Still, she felt foolish, seeing herself through Thomas's eyes. "You never give me credit for common sense."

He smiled a little as his eyes warmed in a knowing look. He'd guessed there was someone. A Janie, who had unsavory friends. Not that circumstances offered her access to a wide pool of so-called respectable acquaintances.

And Abby'd argued the same question too many

times—in heated whispers with her father that were supposed to protect her mom—to discuss it with Thomas now. "You look tired. Let's take care of your back and then you can go to bed when you want."

"Let me help with the dishes."

He acted as if he was afraid to be alone. A chill tiptoed down her spine. "We'll divvy up the chores tomorrow if you think you have to earn your keep, but tonight why don't you sleep? You need it."

That unfamiliar frown knotted his forehead. But he nodded and left the kitchen. Surprised he'd given in, Abby followed. He picked up the first-aid kit from the stairs where he'd left it on the tread beside her keys. In the living room he looked at her furniture, still piled in corners and on the wide hearth. Naturally, it upset his military sense of order.

"Don't even think about it." Abby stopped him before he could offer to help. "I'd worry all night if I let you move this stuff." She patted the coffee table. "Let's get that dressing on your back."

As he sat, he pulled his sweater over his head. She'd expected a bandage, but not several thick squares lumped across his chest beneath the gray T-shirt. She'd spent a year in North Carolina, dreading the news that someone had harmed Thomas.

"I only need your help with my back."

She ducked behind him. They were both more

comfortable without acknowledging his wounds mattered to her.

He took off the T-shirt, revealing fresh scars, nicks in his skin, a harder torso than she remembered—and a large square of layered gauze pads, tattered around the edges.

She reached for the box at his side. "Are you ready?" Without thinking, she brushed the angry red flesh around the adhesive tape. "You're allergic."

"Try to replace it in a slightly different spot. Go ahead and pull, Abby. The tape hurts more than anything else now."

She yanked and was grateful his intake of breath hid her own. A gouge of skin was missing just below his right shoulder blade. Nearly healed, it had been much larger when first inflicted. The tape couldn't possibly hurt more.

Tears burned her eyes. She widened them. Cops didn't cry, and neither did the friend of a man who wanted no pity. Still, she twisted her fingers together, longing to wrap her arms around the soldier who'd once owned her heart. "What in hell happened to you, Thomas?"

His spine couldn't be straighter if he was standing at attention. "Shrapnel from the bomb. I was lucky."

She peered around the walls of the safe haven she'd built, a cozy home filled with photos of only happy times and an afghan her mother had crocheted during a Christmas season when she'd been on an unusually even keel.

Abby stared at Thomas's back, wishing she was the woman to help him, but he still mattered too much. She didn't want to know any more details.

She smeared antibiotic cream over the gash and covered it with a clean bandage. Stick to the business at hand. Sending him to Risa's therapist was the right thing to do. Thomas shuddered as she smoothed on new tape. She pulled back.

"Sorry—I didn't mean to hurt you."

"It's fine." He was a man newly made of stone, and she could barely stand his pain.

"This couldn't have been your fault." She flattened the tape again because she needed to touch him.

He leaned out of her reach, yanking his T-shirt back over his head. Then he stood, wadding his sweater in his fist. "You weren't there."

"I used to wish you'd see how dangerous your job was, but not like this." His mission—he'd always called them "trips"—had obviously driven to the heart of things that mattered most to Thomas.

"I wish I'd done everything differently that day."

"Unless you built the bomb and set it off, you didn't cause the problem."

His eyes, seemingly sightless, stared at her. Thomas wasn't in there anymore. "Good night." The stranger barely moved his lips. "Thank you for letting me stay."

THOMAS PROWLED Abby's house, moving in silence born of training. After previous trips, he'd come home and put on the facade of a normal man. Like anyone else, he rattled down stairs or slapped his hand on the back of a chair. Tonight, he felt as if he were scouting for an enemy.

In the living room, he found a lamp and switched it on. Abby had arranged all her things back into a cozy nest before she'd gone to bed. Puffy chairs and man-size ottomans begged him to rest.

Apple-and-spice pervaded the air. The woman had always loved candles, and the homier they smelled, the more she burned.

He rubbed his nose. Used to dirt and dust and heat, a seat on sand, he couldn't pretend he was at home in Abby's world. He might never again feel normal in the States or in the uncomplicated life he'd taken for granted.

The kind of life he'd fought to preserve.

He'd killed to preserve.

"Damn." His thoughts didn't belong to a sergeant major in the United States Army who'd led his men out of planes and into fire.

He sorted through an ill-stacked pile of books on the coffee table. Here, Martha Stewart ended and a Houston cop took over.

Abby read blood-and-guts mysteries and techni-cal manuals on policing. Thomas almost smiled. Then he turned over the first book to read the back cover and found his heart in his throat as the text promised a kidnapping, a serial-killing artist with a knife and justice for all.

He dropped the book and studied the tidier shelves built into the wall on either side of Abby's fireplace. More to read there.

Abby kept a lot of Agatha Christie. Safe, bloodless puzzles. He fingered each spine.

Miss Marple might be overly calm even for a guy who'd done too much killing. He marked the place from which he plucked a dog-eared copy of Hercule Poirot's adventures on a train. Abby might have a method to her shelving madness, and he didn't want her to find out he'd sunk to reading antiseptic mysteries.

ABBY WOKE TO THE SUNDAY SOUNDS of kids next door calling their puppy. She rolled over, flinging her arms wide in a plea for one more quiet hour.

Then she remembered Thomas.

Concern pulled her onto one elbow. Her clock read 7:12 a.m. She sniffed the air. No coffee.

Thomas had always believed in the restorative properties of strong coffee. He brewed a fresh pot the moment he rose. And Thomas rose. She fought waking with every ounce of strength, but Thomas managed to be totally alert the second he opened his eyes.

She staggered to the bathroom, still drunk with

sleep. Cold water on her face and a strong dose of toothpaste prepared her to meet the day.

She combed her chin-length brown hair, damp around her cheeks and forehead now. A red crease, a gift from her pillow, ran from her nose to her ear.

Makeup? Nah. No need to let Thomas think he still rated cosmetics.

She hoisted the waistband of her pajama pants, straightened her shoulders beneath a tank top dotted with both bleach and paint stains and made for the stairs.

At the bottom she veered toward the kitchen. Listening for footsteps overhead, she made coffee and searched the fridge.

Thomas generally resisted bacon and any other fatty meat product, but she had enough to make him a decent breakfast, and he'd have to live with what he'd termed her bad habits for a day.

"Biscuits." She gathered the fixings her grandmother had taught her to use.

Thomas still hadn't made a sound by the time the biscuits were ready for the oven. She stared at the ceiling. Now she was working on a deadline. A ruined breakfast wouldn't do him a bit of good, but he also needed rest.

Putting off the decision to wake him, she headed down the hall to grab the paper off the sidewalk before the man across the street harvested it. He liked the news fresh every morning in paper form, but he'd embarked on his own form of protest against its increased Sunday cost by stealing her copy.

Stealing from a police officer gave him such satisfaction Abby had stopped explaining right and wrong and just tried to grab it before he could commit his weekly crime. She passed the stairs and was reaching for the alarm system keypad when she realized she'd just passed Thomas, sprawled on the living-room couch.

She backed up. His arm hung off the sofa, and his fingers pointed at a book on the floor. Cold fear shot into her throat as she ran to him.

Opening his eyes, he sprang to his feet. "What?" His hair stood in multidirectional spikes. Death lurked in his eyes and in hands, not fisted, but flexed for action.

"Thomas?" She found a quiet tone. "Everything's okay. You're in Houston."

"God." He pushed his hands over his face and through his hair. "I didn't realize—what time is it?"

"Nearly eight."

"I fell asleep."

"Was your bed uncomfortable?"

"I don't know." He scooped the book off the floor, but not before she noticed Hercule Poirot's well-beloved mustache. One eyebrow went up against her volition. She loved those old mysteries, but Thomas had never been a fan.

"You don't have much to read," he said, his defensive tone spooking her.

"Okay." She glanced at the books on her shelves and the ones he'd obviously looked at and rejected on her coffee table. "I have to get my paper before the guy across the street steals it. Coffee's ready."

"Thanks." He replaced the book. "Your neighbor steals your paper?"

"He tries to."

"Why don't you stop him?"

"I've tried. Now we race for it." She turned to the alarm pad again.

"Abby, did you call your friend?"

"Not yet." She punched in the code and turned the dead bolt on the front door.

"That should be a keyed lock."

His voice, so close, made her jump. He'd crept up on her. "It's fine. Don't you want coffee?" She exited, shutting the door behind her. "Not that you need caffeine."

She peeked over her shoulder, but the door stayed closed. She wouldn't put hearing through it past Thomas.

"I'm going for a run."

Abby looked up from scrubbing a frying pan with too much zeal. They'd shared an unspoken truce over a breakfast neither of them had felt like eating. Abby had finally given up any effort to eat and begun cleaning. Thomas had thrown her a grateful half smile and exited the kitchen as if he was probing escape routes.

Back now, in shorts and sneakers, he looked as if he couldn't wait to free himself from her four walls. If she hadn't seen those shrapnel injuries, it might seem like a Nobel-Prize-winning idea.

"You're not in shape to run," she said.

His look might well kill. "Call your friend."

Yeah. It was almost noon.

"Don't run, Thomas. Walk if you have to, but don't run."

That look impaled her again. He didn't have to tell her he had to run or break something. As he went down the hall, she checked her watch. In twenty minutes she'd hunt him down, and who cared if she humiliated him?

As the front door snicked shut—the man made no noise anymore—she looked for her portable phone. Snagging it from the dining table, she punched in Risa's number.

Closest to Abby in age of the six women who'd bonded during her first tenure at the police academy, Risa was the friend Abby had turned to most often. Risa's voice behind Abby had pushed her over the obstacle course. Risa, with her determined mind, had quizzed her on test questions.

But the shooting that had left Risa under unfounded suspicion had made Abby keep her distance in public. Women who stood together on a mostly male police force could become targets. Abby, who'd spent time in a bad spotlight for leaving the academy the first time, hadn't wanted to make Risa a bigger one. Behind the scenes, she'd tried to make sure Risa knew she could come to her for anything, and Risa had never rejected a call from Abby for advice.

The phone rang three times before someone picked up.

"Risa?"

"Abby, what's going on?"

Her mouth went dry as she tried to bring up the one subject her friends and family considered her fatal flaw.

"I need some help. Thomas came to town last night. You remember him?"

"You mean Riley?" Strain coated her voice.

"He's been wounded and he… Could we meet? I'd rather discuss it in person. It shouldn't take more than half an hour."

"Has he done something to you?" Risa's tone said "let-me-at-him."

"I'm confused, but whole."

Silence equaled doubt, but Risa finally spoke. "Let's meet at the coffee shop near my place. How soon?"

Abby glanced at her watch and then leaned down to look for her boarder, through the windows. "In an hour." If he hadn't shown up by the time she changed clothes, she'd find him. "Thanks, Risa."

"No problem, but are you bringing him?"

"No." He only wanted the therapist's name, not a personal testimonial, and Abby saw no need to join the separate parts of her life. "See you in an hour."

She changed into jeans and a T-shirt, checking outside each time she passed a window. She pulled on her denim jacket as she ran down the stairs and Thomas pushed through the front door. Relief swamped her.

"Don't you ever lock this thing?" he asked.

She smiled—couldn't help it—because she'd pictured him in an unconscious heap somewhere in her neighborhood. "I was about to come look for you." She pointed to the bandage nearest his right shoulder. "You're bleeding."

"Not much."

"You never take care of yourself." Instantly, she wished she'd learn when to keep quiet. What he did to himself was none of her business. "I'm off to meet Risa."

"You couldn't ask for the guy's name over the phone?"

"I could." She shook her keys in the palm of her hand. "But I want her to understand, and this feels like a face-to-face request."

"She might turn you down because you're asking for me?"

"A lot of men still don't want women on the force, and they point at someone like me as an excuse to keep us out. I don't want Risa or anyone else I work with to be confused about why I'm trying to help you."

"I still don't get this. We planned to get married."

He said it so easily, as if the memories didn't matter. Maybe they always would to her. Maybe first love left a deep scar when it went bad. "A lot of the guys at work think I didn't deserve a second chance."

"Did Risa help you get back in the academy?"

"That wasn't her job. Standing up for me might have hurt her career, but I knew I could count on her." She grabbed a bottle of water from the fridge and took it back to him. "Here."

He took it, but then stared at it in his hand. "Thanks." He wiped sweat off his forehead. "You don't have to coddle me."

"Even in January, you should drink lots of water after a run here. The humidity'll kill you." At the kitchen door, she remembered his back. "Do you want me to help you change—"

"No." He said it fast.

"Fine." Shallow breaths helped her avoid his musky scent. It reminded her of shared postrun showers and passion that felt good, even in memory. She put that out of her head. No one could be twenty-one and foolish all her life. "My extra keys are on that peg beside the fridge if you decide to go out."

He caught the small flashlight that dangled from

her key chain, a troubled apology on his face. He might have touched her, but her key chain was the only commitment he could afford.

"I don't mean to hurt your feelings, and I'm grateful for what you're doing, but how can I ask for more? Even simple things."

His thready voice seduced her. With the unfinished past between them, she still remembered how wanting him felt. "I understand." She tugged back on the chain. "Risa's waiting."

She stepped into the garage, but her hand shook as she punched the remote to open the door. She hurried to her car and jabbed her key into the ignition.

She had to compose herself or Risa would realize Thomas still counted more than he should. She felt calmer by the time she parked in front of the glass-fronted coffee shop.

Abby hurried inside, missing the times when all her friends had gathered in a crisis. Risa stood to get Abby's attention from a table on the far side of the little building. The sex-crimes detective had seated herself in a spot that allowed visual access to the other customers and the parking lot outside. A man might not be as careful. A woman had more to prove, and Risa had already proven herself again and again to the Houston PD.

Abby smiled to hide tension so overwhelming her teeth hurt from gritting them. Risa's hug eased her nervousness.

"Whatever he wants is serious?"

"Yeah." She appreciated Risa's quick understanding. "Thanks for coming."

"Sure." They both sat, Abby with her back to the room.

A server approached their table. Abby ordered coffee, glancing at her watch.

"You can't leave him alone?" Risa asked.

"You want to know the truth? I tend to mother everyone. Thomas is making me wish I could stop."

"You wouldn't be yourself. Tell me how I can help."

"One of Thomas's assignments went wrong, and he has some problems he needs to handle before he can go back to North Carolina."

Risa reached for a sugar packet, which she smoothed between her fingers. "What kind of wrong?"

"You're always on the job."

Her friend's expression asked, "What else?"

Abby grimaced. "Some of his men were killed, along with a woman and her children. He feels responsible."

"I didn't shoot Luke, Abby." Risa placed the sugar in its plastic dish. "And even if I understood what Thomas feels, I wouldn't know what to say to him."

"I know, but the department made you see a therapist."

Risa looked disgusted. "That's time I'll never get back."

"He didn't help?"

"He couldn't. I didn't do the thing he tried to treat me for."

Their server arrived with two coffees on a tray. Abby reached for one cup.

Risa took hers. "The Army provides medical care."

"They consider him cured. I can't get much out of Thomas, but if he sees a therapist now that the Army thinks he's well, he'll lose his job."

"Are you safe with him? Do you know how these people died?"

"He'd never hurt me." Not on purpose anyway, and not physically, as Risa meant. Abby set down her coffee. "He's upset and he's reverted to training, as we would. He sneaked into town. He walks around without making a sound, as if someone's after him. He says he can't lead his men until he's sure he won't make a mistake."

"Maybe he should resign."

"You didn't leave your job. I came running back to mine." Abby shook her head. "He's as tied to his work as any of us. He won't leave the Army."

"I'll give you the therapist's name, but who knows if he's good?"

"Would he refuse to turn over patient records?" Abby didn't have to explain Thomas couldn't afford that.

"I don't know. He took the department line all the way with me. What about Liam? If you ask, he'll keep the secret."

"I suggested Liam. Thomas said no."

Risa tilted her head. "You know that's bad. He shouldn't care about your ex-husband. Don't get involved with a damaged guy who hasn't let you go."

Abby linked her fingers. "He was never a monster—we just weren't supposed to be together. I have to help him if I can, but I'm no fool."

"You go too far to help people, and you've already let him back in." Risa's concern softened the harsh words.

"I thought he was my future when I was twenty-one, but I got smarter. I'd help anyone who needed me this much."

"Your mother's problems conditioned you to jump in with both feet when someone can't handle his life, but when are you going to learn self-preservation?" Risa took a pad and pen from her purse. "Here's the name and number." She jotted down the information and then looked up. "Look at me, Abby. Don't walk into jeopardy."

Strong coffee smells and too much honesty made Abby's ears ring, as if her blood pressure were shooting sky high. "I'm helping him. Thomas will get better and go home. I'll finally have a chance to say a real goodbye. Maybe we'll get each other out of our systems."

"I'm afraid you're lying to yourself."

A reluctant smile escaped Abby. "I haven't done that since I left North Carolina." She scooped up the piece of paper and stuffed it into her back pocket. Then she grabbed a few bucks out of her jacket. "This is for the bill. I'm sorry I have to run." She leaned down to hug her quiet, confident friend. "Thank you, for the number and for worrying about me, but you don't have to."

"You won't put yourself first."

"You and the others"—their academy friends— "have suggested that before." Arguing now was just as pointless as it had been six years ago. No one else could see the ties between her and Thomas. "What do you hear from everyone else lately?"

"Lucy and I are patching things up, and I've talked to Crista. We're working out our problems." She toasted their own meeting with her coffee cup. "You and I talk. Maybe this was bound to happen. Six different women with changing lives and careers. And Catherine's our boss. She can't afford to look as if she's partial to a few of her employees."

"I guess. I've seen Mei to say hello, and I spoke with Lucy a few weeks ago," Abby said. "Crista helped me with someone on the street one day, but I wish we could all be as close as we were."

"You'll see me plenty if you let Thomas hurt you again."

Abby grinned. She always took care of herself, but

she couldn't resent her friend's concern in the least. She touched the pocket where she'd tucked the number Risa had given her. "This is all I'm offering him."

CHAPTER THREE

AFTER THOMAS SHOWERED and changed his bandages, he sat at the kitchen table with Abby's newspaper. His mind roamed as the words wandered on the page, until Abby's cat put his paws onto the edge of the chair.

"What?"

The cat blinked its green eyes.

"I don't know where your food is."

Herb meowed and then bumped his nose against Thomas's hand. At the moist contact, Thomas stood. Herb dropped to the floor again and inspected his food dish before lapping some water. Thomas returned the paper to its original folds and left the kitchen and the cat.

Back in the living room, he turned on the Sunday talk shows, but the politicians bugged him. Herb strolled in and curled up on the shiny floor.

Back to Poirot. The book worked until he realized he'd been staring at Abby's crown molding for uncountable minutes.

Another run might look odd to the neighbors, but

he needed it. As he stood, the doorbell rang and Herb fled, his back paws scrambling for purchase.

"That was easy." He needed no new best friends, not even Herb.

Through the front door's brass-encircled peephole he saw a man who looked older than he should. But Abby's father hadn't softened. Nor had his wife, a slightly taller, more studious version of her only child.

Her pinched expression had always made him think something was wrong. For a while, he'd even wondered if John hit his wife. Then Abby had explained, and he understood—now better than ever.

She was anxious because she wasn't always sure she walked in step with the people in her life. Illness put her at a distance and at a disadvantage.

John Carlton adjusted the black tie at his white collar. Elaine, thin to the point of fragility, smoothed her belted pink dress. Steeling themselves for a Sunday visit. Thomas opened the door.

Abby's parents stared at him as if he'd broken out of prison.

"What the hell are you doing here?" John asked.

Nice talk from a fully tenured professor of all the best dead languages. He caught his wife as she reeled to the edge of the porch.

"Dr. Carlton." Thomas barely stopped himself from reaching for her, too. "And Dr. Carlton." He offered to shake John's hand, but the other man stared at his open palm, too antagonistic to respond.

With a ninety-nine percent phony smile, Thomas stood aside to offer them the run of their daughter's home. John's hostility barely nicked his conscience. "Come in. I expect Abby back soon."

"I asked why you were here." John took Elaine's arm to help her over the threshold. "Where's our daughter?

"Did you break in?" Her question made Thomas look at her twice.

"No." He kept his voice gentle. Anything could destroy the balance she maintained with so much effort. As the man who'd broken her daughter's heart, he probably counted as a threat. "Abby offered me a place to stay while I'm on leave." They looked at him, calling him a liar without saying a single word. "Visiting a few friends," he added.

"Why stay with Abby?" John asked.

"You know your daughter. She can't hold a grudge." A wise soldier used his enemy's worst fears against him, and they'd be more upset with Abby if they knew the truth.

"I need a drink." Elaine looked toward the living room in search of a snakebite cure. "How about you, John?"

"I'll get it." Thomas followed Elaine's thirsty glance and found liquor in a cabinet beside the doorway. He poured bourbon for John, a scotch for Elaine and handed over both glasses, denying himself a drink he badly wanted.

"Honey, let me take your coat." John peeled Elaine's coat off her shoulders and then shucked off his own jacket. "When did you call Abby, Riley?"

"Thomas." He and Abby should have cooked up a story. He kept it simple. "Not too long ago. Another drink?"

The Carltons lifted their full glasses in unison. Elaine sipped, her stare pinning Thomas to the floor. He suspected she was making up a worst-case scenario to explain his being in Abby's house.

"You don't drink now?" John asked.

"You're asking if I have a problem?"

"You will if you upset my daughter."

Who said professors weren't tough? "That's the last thing I want, sir."

The front door burst open. Abby came in, tossing her coat at the stairs. "I have a name, Thomas."

"A name for what?" Elaine asked.

Abby stopped, looking from face to face to face. She gave an extra keen glance to her mother, who quickly sipped her drink. Abby smiled apologetically, but her eyes asked Thomas why he'd let her parents in.

"An old friend of Thomas's told him about—"

She dried up. Thomas jumped in. "A restaurant. A place I'd forgotten, but one of Abby's friends knew it, too."

"What place?" John asked.

Abby hesitated, and anyone could see she was thinking too hard. "The Golden Hind. It's a pub."

"What are you two trying to hide?" Raw fear crossed John Carlton's face before he drained his drink. "You haven't married him this time?"

"Dad." Abby asked him to stop with her tone of voice. "Don't you know the inquisition's over?"

He stared at his glass. "Your mother and I can't forget what this man did to you."

"All in the past."

"When a man breaks your child's heart and turns her into someone you hardly know, you can't stay out of it." Elaine stepped up to Thomas. "I can't imagine how you found the nerve to show up after all these years, but I'm glad to tell you exactly what we think of you."

"I don't blame you." She didn't have to convince him. He hadn't turned out to be the man either he or Abby had expected, and he'd let her down.

Abby broke up the confrontation. "Thomas, will you give me a few minutes with my parents?"

"Sure, but don't try to make them be nice. I think you deserved better, too." He climbed the stairs and closed his door to give her family privacy.

"THOMAS AND I ARE FRIENDS, nothing more. You're not allowed to grill him." Blood roared in her ears. Six years too late, he was contrite. How could he talk like that in front of her mom and dad?

The last thing she needed was for her mom to think she and Thomas might be starting over. Abby's breakup had pitched her mother into one of the deepest holes she'd ever had. Abby's sadness had somehow transferred to her mother, but Abby had recovered first.

She and her father had spent months dragging her mom out of her dark-curtained bedroom, trying to make her believe Abby wasn't going to die from the loss of the man she'd loved. Her mother's depression had never been based on logic.

Abby tugged her parents toward the hall. Her father tried to resist and spilled the last drops from his glass. His gaze followed the liquid to the floor with regret.

"Hold on, Abby. It's about time we had our say with that guy."

Abby took his arm again. "You're trying to protect me, but I'm fine. Thomas is on vacation and he wanted to say he was sorry about the past. Apparently, serving in the desert makes you want to tie up loose ends." She led them to the kitchen, trying to seem normal. "Have you eaten? Let's cook something."

"Clean up your father's spilled drink, Abby." Her mother peered over her shoulder. "Someone will slip."

"I'm more concerned Herb might find it." Abby shot a quick look up and down the hall. "I'll take care of it while you two get comfy in the kitchen. Dad, you can fire up the grill. We'll sit in the yard and watch the birds, and you'll leave the dead past alone."

"If your past is dead, why let him stay?" Her father stopped their little procession. "You still care for that man."

"Dad." She managed not to glance guiltily toward Thomas's room, but she abandoned any pretense of gently assisting them. She strong-armed her parents out of Thomas's earshot and sat them both at the kitchen table. "I care for a lot of people. You two, for instance, but I've made some smart decisions, too."

"You can't resist the bad ones." Her mother, still clutching a little bit of her drink, finished it off. "You had every advantage. Maybe we aren't rich, but you never wanted food or clothing. We gave you an excellent education. You could have gone anywhere to take your master's and doctorate. Instead, you—you join the police force, and then you go after that man. And if that wasn't enough you let him dump you and then come back for a second shot at you."

"Mom—"

Abby appealed to her father. Medication had ended her mother's last episode about four months earlier, but effective medication only convinced Elaine that she didn't need to take it. The vicious cycle had ruled their lives, and it was normal for many victims of bipolar disease.

"I'm not sick, John. You have to listen to me about Thomas." Her gaze a little wild, she wrapped her hands around Abby's. "I recognize a guy in trouble. He shows no emotion. He's watchful—afraid someone will notice he's two steps behind the rest of the world. I know exactly what's going on with him. I just want to know why."

Abby stared at her father. They tried so hard to protect her mom, they forgot she understood when she was sick. Abby didn't want to lie, but telling them what had happened to Thomas would only convince them they were right.

"Leave it alone, Mom. Nothing's wrong."

"You've barely recovered from the last time you broke up." Abby tried to deny it, but Elaine tightened her hands. "I can't watch you throw away the little stability you've regained on the same man who—"

"The little stability?" The words stung like a slap. "How long have you been holding that in?"

"Our family flaw is the compulsion to pretend everything's fine—just fine, but not this time. Thomas could ruin your life again."

"I'm not unstable." It was her worst fear.

"You couldn't keep a job when you first came back from North Carolina."

"Elaine." John eased her away from Abby, and Abby shot him a look of relief. "You'll scare the girl."

Suddenly, her kitchen seemed small, and she felt anywhere but at home in the haven she'd built so carefully. This was a variation of the scenes they'd replayed since the first time her father had left to teach a class, worried because her mom wasn't capable of caring for her.

"I'm not a girl, Dad. And, Mom, I took odd jobs while I tried to get back into the academy. My English degree didn't offer a lot of choices."

"I remember those delightful days when you delivered pizza."

"I also edited your church newsletter, Mother."

"That man stole your self-confidence."

"I wanted my old job back, and I had to pay my bills until I got it." She refused to admit she'd drifted between go-nowhere jobs, unable to focus on her old life. "And if I hadn't gone to North Carolina with Thomas I'd still wonder if I'd given up on him because he lived so far away. We found out we're a train wreck together."

"So why'd he come back?"

"To see friends. I'm letting him stay with me. End of subject." She found an extra inch of spine. "Or I have to send you home."

As if on cue, they both eyed their empty glasses, her father too wary of causing waves to argue, her mother surrendering. Abby turned her watch over. "I've never seen you two touch the hard stuff before four."

"Not in six years anyway," her mom said.

Abby let it go, her mind on Thomas, who might be packing after her parents' spectacular welcome. "I'll mix margaritas. Why don't you wait for me on the deck?"

Her garden, an oasis for hummingbirds and butterflies, was her mom's favorite part of the house. "No margarita for me. Just tea," her mother said. "Sweet, if you have it."

"Aah, from hard liquor to sugar. That's more like my folks."

Her father lagged behind as her mother went to the shaded deck. "Come here." He hugged her. "Have we turned you into a loner? I was thinking—you broke up with Thomas, married Liam a couple of years later, but since the divorce, you don't see anyone."

Abby hugged him back. "I'm happy, and everything's fine. Don't worry."

He let her go. "I'm looking out for you."

"Shh." She glanced through the screen, sniffing the sweet, perfumed air. "I promise, Thomas won't stay long."

"Why does he have to stay here?"

"He's a friend—nothing for you all to be so upset about."

"A lifetime in our family topped off with a hint of psychological training has turned you into a reckless woman. You can't handle everyone's problems."

She sighed, starting to get impatient. Her dad knew her too well to be fooled. She urged him toward the door. "Go talk to Mom. You know how to make her feel better."

He went reluctantly.

She closed the door and filled a saucepan with water and tea bags. Then, after a swift glance at her parents, their heads bent together as they rocked on the porch swing, she hurried down the hall to find Thomas back in the living room. Standing at the windows, he stared into the yard.

"I should go." He turned his head. "I don't want to make more trouble."

"You heard all that?" He surprised her. "You're not an eavesdropper."

Outside, a child yelled. Thomas nodded toward the sound. "I heard your voices. You don't have to listen to know when the people are upset."

"They'll get used to you being here."

His smile took a long time to appear, and the slow curve started an inappropriate quiver in the pit of her stomach. She placed her hand across her belly, a barricade between him and her. Forbidden fruit could be deadly.

"They'd never get used to me being anywhere."

He might be right. "Are you hungry?" She tried to make their relationship feel more normal. "We're cooking on the grill."

Again, he smiled, but he didn't seem to mean it. "Do they know you're asking me?"

She rubbed her hands down her arms. Making an alliance with Thomas against her parents seemed disloyal. "A quiet meal might reassure them."

"I can still man a barbecue."

"Good. You can help my dad. If I gave you directions to the grocery store, would you pick up ribs?"

"Gladly."

He looked grateful to escape, and she practically danced at the thought of a break. Thomas's tension seemed to have stuck itself to every corner of her house.

He went upstairs for his car keys while she wrote out directions and a shopping list. His walk, as they met at the bottom of the stairs seemed more tentative than usual.

He might be tired. He might be in pain.

She didn't ask. She didn't want to get any more involved with a man so troubled.

"Be careful," she said but wished she hadn't. His shoulders, once stereotypically broad and protective, now carried wounds that affected him inside and out. He needed her now, and their bond was changing. In two days they knew each other more intimately than they had in six years before.

Thomas looked down, somber. She smiled warily. She didn't want him worrying about her.

"I'm sorry about…" He glanced down the hall, toward the kitchen.

"You don't have to be." She shrugged. "Separate problems."

His soft laugh warmed her. "I'm one and they're the other?" he asked.

"Better get those ribs." She opened the door. "I'm starving."

"I won't be long." He brushed his palm over her

shoulder. "And thanks again. I had no reason to expect you'd go so far to help me."

"Please don't thank me anymore." No big catastrophe loomed on their horizon. They just had to find a good therapist who could help him before her parents reached meltdown. Abby took his hand. "You've been unfinished business in my life for too long. I ran when I should have faced you."

Regret made him frown. "I wish you had."

His unexpected answer did funny things to her heartbeat. She felt as if she were hanging in midair. Would he have tried to talk her out of leaving? Would she have let him?

His skin suddenly seemed too hot against hers. She let him go. She had to forget he'd been her lover. Nothing changed the problems that had split them up.

IN THE GROCERY STORE, surrounded by strangers, Thomas felt at ease for the first time since Abby had seen him. Nobody in the store cared what he did next. No one looked at him as if he was on the verge of a breakdown. No one even looked at him twice.

He pushed a metal basket, going nowhere at any speed. The more time he gave Abby and her parents, the better off they'd all be.

On the way back through her quiet neighborhood, he wondered where all the activity had gone. Even her house looked still. He carried the bags up the walkway and turned the doorknob. The door opened. Abby had left it unlocked.

He muttered beneath his breath as he carted the groceries to the kitchen. The woman would never pay attention to her own security.

He walked through the house, hearing only silence. Abby and her parents must still be in the yard. Just as he began to unpack the food, someone walked on the floor overhead.

In his room.

He spun, his hand going to the hip where he usually carried his sidearm. His fingers curved around jeans and an empty belt loop. Swearing, he leaned into the kitchen window to find the Carltons. Abby and her father were talking down by the hedge. He couldn't see Elaine, but they must be speaking to her.

Thomas ran down the hall and took the stairs, fighting off memories of another house, textured walls, rough against his flexed fingertips, low voices and death waiting, death longing to bite his men when they reached the top.

Shaking his head to empty out the memories, he edged down the hall. He stopped just this side of Abby's guest-room door.

Someone was inside, tossing his belongings as if noise was part of any good search. The door stood slightly open. He shoved it with one hand and charged, fist first.

Elaine Carlton jumped back from his open bag so

fast she tripped over her feet, falling inside the closet. He didn't trust himself to help her. If she'd been her husband, he might have tossed her through the window.

"What's up?" He controlled his breathing, ignored the rapid pumping of his heart.

Fear pinched her face, but she straightened and stepped from the closet, pulling her shoulder seams even. "I want to know why you're here. I don't believe what you and my daughter told us. She can't resist a hard-luck story, but not even Abby would let you visit after the way you two broke up."

"I told you I'm sorry about that, but you can't go rifling through my things." He held still, not trusting his own reflexes.

Footsteps at his back made him jump. He felt like an idiot. When he turned, he found Abby staring at him as if she expected a crisis.

"Are you all right?" Her tone made him a victim in her care.

"Great." He pulled his bag across the bed. Elaine must have gone at his things with an eggbeater. "Sorry." He couldn't look at Abby as he apologized for his short temper. "I'm fine."

She went to Elaine. "Even cops need a warrant, Mom."

"Who'd convict me?" Elaine dared her daughter to say anything else. "I just want to know the truth about why he's here."

"Imagine finding Thomas up to his elbows in your clothes." She was so upset, he decided not to mention her mother had fallen into the closet, but not elbows first. "Now come with me and don't snoop in here unless he invites you." She sounded more worried than angry. "Not that I see Thomas asking you back."

"It's okay," he said.

Both women stared as if he'd sprouted a spare head.

"I see her point."

"I'm not mentally incompetent." Elaine looked as annoyed as he'd been with Abby's pity. The full force of her doubt was in her brown eyes, so much like her daughter's. "I have a point because you ruined my daughter's life once already."

"Mother, I might want Thomas to think it didn't hurt to leave him behind." Her blush deepened. "The past is over, and you don't need to spell it out for him."

She'd hurt him leaving, and he was weak enough to be glad it hadn't been easy for her, either. But she was right about the past. He'd come for help, not a reunion. He moved toward the closet. "If you don't mind, I'll put my stuff away."

"We'll see you downstairs." Abby waited, and her mother passed her like a sulky child. "If you still want to eat with us."

"None of this is a problem," he said. "Don't worry, and don't try to make Elaine feel guilty for taking care of you."

As soon as her mother was on the other side of the door, Abby pushed it shut.

"You'll hurt her feelings," he said, surprised.

"I know, but are you all right? I'm sorry she searched your things."

He nodded, exasperation coursing through his body like a muscle ache. Feeling anything was good after so long. "I'm with Elaine. You look at us as if you don't know what we'll do next."

"How can I help it?" She shook her head as if pretty much anything *could* happen.

"Let's stick with reality. She'll want to know what we're talking about, and I thought we'd agreed to keep my secrets between us."

"Everything's going to be fine. Mom just went too far."

He wanted to hold her—promise nothing bad would happen because she'd taken him in. Only, he couldn't. "I'll search your stuff later. We'll call it even." Abby didn't get the joke. He grimaced. "If you don't open that door, your mom's going to write the Joint Chiefs about me." But then she did, and he reached for her. "Abby, wait."

She turned.

"Is she still there?"

She shook her head.

"Did your friend give you a name?"

"The therapist. Yeah." She searched both front jean pockets, drawing unnecessary attention to her softly rounded hips before she found a slip of paper in her back pocket. "Here."

"I'll call and leave a message."

"Maybe we can get a group rate." Affection softened her dry tone. No amount of resentment or worry had ever dimmed her love for her parents. "Come down when you finish your call. And thanks for being nice to my mom."

She left, and he stared at the empty space where she'd stood. He closed his eyes. He'd never put her in danger again, not from anyone who might want him dead. Not from himself.

He opened the paper she'd handed him and sat on the bed beside the phone. A smooth voice invited him to leave a message on a machine. Just as Thomas opened his mouth, the same voice cut in.

"Dr. Austen, here."

Thomas looked down. Leo Austen. "Dr. Austen, my name is Thomas Riley. An officer from the Houston PD gave me your name. I'd like to discuss a problem."

A short silence conveyed reluctance. "I only answered my phone because I expected a call from my car detailer. I really don't work on weekends, but why don't you tell me what you need." From the doctor's side of the conversation pens and paper rustled. "You're a policeman?"

"No." He didn't identify himself. The man had only answered his phone because he'd thought his car was ready. Thomas needed someone who wouldn't put off a prospective patient with unwilling silence and a caution that he didn't work on weekends.

"Hello?" The doctor's tone made Thomas think he was checking his watch. "I could leave my girl a note to call you tomorrow and set up an appointment."

Thomas frowned. His "girl?" Suddenly Abby seemed wise, suggesting he shouldn't see a stranger. Austen might be a decent doctor, but his manner hardly threw a desperate man a rope.

"No, thanks," Thomas said. He crushed the doctor's name in his hand. Damn it to hell. "I'll call back." Unless he forced himself to approach the last psychologist he'd willingly see. He'd rather give a full report of his doubts to his captain than spill his guts to Abby's ex-husband.

CHAPTER FOUR

ABBY CALLED LIAM first thing next morning. Already in his office, he answered the phone personally. "What's up?" he asked.

"Where's Roberta?" His assistant usually answered.

"It's seven-thirty. She's not here yet."

"Why are you in so early?"

"Abby, did you call for a reason? I didn't know you cared so much about my work habits."

"Funny." He never let her get away with much.

"You sound nervous. You've picked up someone you want me to see pro bono?"

She blinked at the kitchen wall six inches in front of her face. He knew her too well, and she'd never appreciated his talent for reading her mind. "I have someone I'd like you to talk to. But not for free."

"Who?"

She took a deep breath and plunged in. "Thomas Riley."

Liam's silence fell as thick and heavy as wet snow. "Thomas Riley?" He layered more silence into the conversation. Abby waited, too. "I don't suppose you know two men by that name?"

"No." It was pointless to assure him yet again that Thomas wasn't the reason she hadn't loved him enough to stay married.

"What's wrong with him?" His massive leather chair rumbled. "And what's wrong with you that you'd dare ask me to see him?"

"He's been serving in the desert, and he lost some of his men in combat. As for why I'd ask, I believe in you."

"Abby—" he already sounded tired, despite the early hour "—don't butter me up."

"You're the doctor I'd choose if I had a problem. You can't help caring for your patients, and I know you won't expose Thomas's secrets to anyone else."

"Huh?"

"You wouldn't turn over his files, no matter who asked for them."

"What's he done?"

Subtlety had never been her strongest character trait. "Will you see him, Liam?"

"I—" He gave in. "I was going to argue, but why? I never win with you. Is this guy really in trouble?"

"I wouldn't ask if he wasn't." Abby's shoulders twitched. "I know I'm asking too much."

"I can hear how upset you are and that you want to help, but I have personal feelings against him."

"You're too decent to let them get in the way."

He was silent again. "You like me too much, Abby. Makes you wonder why we couldn't make our marriage work."

Her ex-husband's sarcasm twisted in Abby's stomach. They loved each other, but not in the right way.

"We're good at friendship."

"Tell him I'll call when I'm on my way."

"Thanks," she said, but Liam, exasperated, had already hung up.

ABBY FINALLY PICKED UP her keys and coat and a uniform on hangars. "If I wait any longer, I'll be late."

Thomas nearly thanked her. Her hovering made waiting for Liam Webster even worse. "Go on. I'll introduce myself." He opened the door for her, glad she wouldn't witness his first reaction to her ex-husband.

She drifted toward the threshold. "Try not to offend him. He's liable to be touchy about you." Her uniform caught on the doorknob, and she turned to disentangle it.

Her nervousness was out of character. She and Liam might have divorced each other, but she still felt plenty for him. "If Liam's as touchy as you, I don't stand a chance."

"I'm overreacting. Between my parents' visit and the thought of Liam treating you, I'm almost glad to go to work. My house is full of stress."

"Don't cops secretly love stress?" he asked.

"I'm a cop because I can't help getting involved

with other peoples' problems, but I like to keep them outside my own four walls." Her grin acknowledged her own imperfections. She hurried down the walkway, sun glinting off her dark brown hair, her step light, yet determined.

Had she been like this when they were engaged? Unafraid to talk about her flaws? Troubled, but determined to help him conquer his? Why had he pushed her away?

He opened his mouth, her name on his lips, but a cool wind brought him to his senses. Down the street, a car alarm sounded, and Thomas jumped.

He'd be lucky if he ever understood his new ability to fear, much less learned to deal with it. He hadn't come here to fix things with Abby. His duty lay in North Carolina with his men.

He went back inside, locked the door and put on coffee in the kitchen. Forget about Abby. He had to greet her ex-husband-psychologist on a house call. At last, the doorbell rang.

Using the peephole, he stole a look at the man who'd replaced him in Abby's life. Liam Webster had replaced him in Abby's heart. As if Thomas had never owned a place there at all.

The other man surprised him. Hardly taller than Abby, he wore glasses, and his crew cut emphasized a hairline that had begun to recede at the temples.

Thomas had expected Superman, but Dr. Webster looked his part, a careful, well-educated guy who devoted his professional life to helping people recover from trauma and trouble. Not taller, stronger or better looking. Maybe Abby had chosen him to make herself forget a man who was almost his complete opposite.

Thomas resented him even more.

He opened the door. Liam looked him over, with the same interest Thomas had felt. Thomas gave the other man time to draw conclusions. It was only fair.

"Good morning." Abby's ex-husband extended his hand. "I'm Liam Webster."

"Morning, Doctor." Thomas shook. Disturbing images of Abby with Liam popped into his head, and he fought an urge to clench his fist around the other man's fingers. He stood aside, curbing his own jealousy. He had to stop thinking about Abby. This therapist might be his best hope for returning to his job.

"Liam. Call me Liam." He carried no briefcase. Or even a notepad. And he made no move to accept Thomas's silent invitation inside.

"Come in."

"Okay." He shucked his jacket.

Thomas waited for him to take paper out of his pocket. "I thought you guys took notes."

"Not when we want to make sure no one else sees them."

"Good thinking. The living room's over here." He stopped. "Maybe you know that?"

"I never lived here."

"I wasn't asking." But he had been.

Liam obviously didn't believe him. "Let's agree not to lie to each other."

"All right. I wanted to know, but your relationship with Abby is none of my business."

Liam looked him right in the eye. "You had a relationship. We had a marriage."

His unexpected emphasis pulled Thomas to a stop. Bitterness coursed through his body. It was definitely time for a run—straight to North Carolina. "I'm glad you agreed to see me, but did Abby browbeat you into it?"

Liam tried to hold his gaze, but Thomas was better at facing down an enemy. Liam pressed his fingers to the nosepiece on his glasses. "I wouldn't have given in if I didn't want to help you." He shut the door. "Do I smell coffee?"

"I'll get you a cup."

"We'll start talking while you pour."

Thomas took the hint. Might as well get it over with. He agreed. In the kitchen he took out cups and cream and sugar and passed Liam coffee. They looked at each other, aloof as only two men who've loved the same woman can be.

Liam looked away again, his gaze sweeping the pale lemon-and-blue kitchen, the gleaming blue tile counters and fresh fruit on the table.

"Do you mind if we talk in the living room?" he asked.

"Fine." The kitchen felt too homey to Thomas, as well. Abby's personality clung. He was too aware of her here, and he assumed Liam felt the same.

The other man waited at the living-room door. Thomas glanced at him, guessing his choice of seating arrangement was a test. He hadn't played these kinds of games since early in his Special Ops training. He sat in a large, leather Windsor chair. Room for one. No room to share.

Liam sprawled on the sofa. "Why did you want to see me?" "Of all people" hung, implicit in the question.

"Abby considered you my best bet."

"For telling off the government if they ask about you?"

"Yes."

"But you still love Abby so you tried someone else first."

"Still love her?"

"Don't you? Why did you run to her first?"

"I knew what she'd been doing—the Crisis Intervention Team. She's always helped her mom. I hoped she could help me." He suddenly remembered he didn't have to put up with this shit. "Is this relevant?"

Liam started, but then slowly crossed one leg over the other as if he'd only moved to adopt a more relaxed posture.

It was answer enough.

"Maybe Abby's off-limits for us." She'd be thrilled with the way Thomas had treated Liam so far. He'd better back down, even if he had to bite through his cheek and punch out a couple of her walls.

Liam took a pen from his pocket and pushed it behind his ear. "We'd better not talk about her. I'm only human, and I've resented you for a while. I thought you should know."

"Can you be objective?"

"I think so or I wouldn't have come this morning."

"You have no reason to worry about Abby and me. I didn't come back to start anything with her. I need help because of—something that happened during my last assignment."

Liam studied Thomas. "Abby says you've been in the desert?"

He nodded, unable to speak now that he had the ear of someone who had to know everything he could tell. As he moved back into that day, rage held him numb and terrified, a stranger to himself. He wasn't this man. Nothing frightened him enough to keep him from acting.

Liam cut through the haze. "Tell me."

"Just like that?" The man had never caused an innocent human being's death, had never realized he didn't want to pull another trigger even though his job was to fight without passion.

Liam narrowed his eyes. "Tell me why you think it's still happening."

"What?" Thomas snapped his head up. If it were still happening, he'd have left a trail of bodies from D.C. to Houston, just to prove he could still kill.

"How often do you relive the battle that killed your friends? I see it in your fists. You're trying to hide the shaking, but you couldn't help dribbling coffee on the counter. You have a pulse that beats on the side of your throat. You constantly lick your lips. Your mouth is always dry. All physical symptoms I could blame on our conversation about my ex-wife, except you look so exhausted I suspect you're terrified to sleep."

"Wait."

Normally, men followed Thomas's orders. Liam didn't. "You're guilty." He sat back. "Maybe you think you should die at least once for every man you lost."

Thomas resisted a feeble urge to cover his face. "You're either good or you're psychic."

"If I were psychic I wouldn't have needed any training, and Abby wouldn't have…" He let the thought die.

Thomas eyed him sharply. "What?" But he knew. "You'd have known how to keep Abby happy?"

"You're a bit psychic, yourself." At Liam's dry tone, Thomas trusted him more—until he thought the other man might be taking a shortcut to gain his trust. Liam waved his hand to clear the air. "Forget Abby. Tell me what happened to your men."

"Eight of us. We were a team. We were together, almost more than we were with our families. We thought as one body, and we'd run similar missions—" he scratched the back of his neck "—I don't know how many times. Their wives and children trusted me to bring them back. But they were well trained. They waited for my signal."

He couldn't admit they crowded around him in every mirror he passed. They haunted each restless night. The three who'd died had forgiven him in sleep he hated more than waking.

It was his own wishful thinking that they should hate him as much as he loathed himself.

"Tell me what you're thinking, Thomas."

He licked his lips. "I need water."

"You think you do because you're back in the desert. Drink the coffee. Obviously, you made it."

Thomas lifted his head in a silent *why?*

"Abby's isn't this good."

"She doesn't add enough grounds." He stroked the bandage beneath his collarbone. "This was the only wound I felt," he said. "My team was sent to snatch a cleric. You wouldn't know his name. Our superiors thought he could help us talk to the local people. He saw we weren't there to take over, and he was willing to say so, but he couldn't come to us. We had to take him out of enemy territory." He reached for his mug, swigged the coffee. Tried to duck the past. "There were stairs. Miles and miles of stairs. We knew the house was too quiet. Thank God I left men at the doors on the ground floor." He looked at Liam. "They didn't die."

"Neither did you."

Yeah. Scourge him with the worst part of his guilt. "Three guys came with me. Corporal Teague had a wife and a baby. Private Davis got engaged the day before we left the States. Corporal Bates only had his parents." He felt sick. "And they only had him."

"What happened?"

"We climbed in the dark. We had night vision goggles, but I pressed my free hand to the wall." He flattened his palm against the wooden table at his side, trying to feel the inlay's pattern. "The stucco was cool. Surprisingly cool. It felt good against my skin because we were always so damn hot. I listened. To hear anything. My men did the same. A sound meant someone knew we'd come. That our intelligence was wrong and someone had set us up for an ambush." A breath rattled down his throat. "The cleric should have had guards, but he didn't. It looked suspicious, but we had to go on. The stairs narrowed as we reached the top. They ended at a closed door. A dark hole against pale walls."

His voice broke. How many times had he opened that door in his nightmares?

"Thomas?"

"No. I can see that far, but I don't want to go on."

He didn't care how feeble he sounded. "I'm not stupid enough to make that mistake again."

"Tell me. Humans make mistakes."

"Shove the platitudes." He yanked his hand off the table and scraped it across his mouth. "You sit here in your safe little world, thinking you're so smart because you recognize post-traumatic stress disorder before I say a word. Well, I understand it, too. I know the statistics. I could even kill someone else because I can't forget the mistake I made. Our intelligence was wrong. How the hell could anyone be so stupid?" His chest ached. He pressed his hand to the wound that burned as if shrapnel were still digging into his skin. He lowered his head. Bile climbed his throat.

"What happened? Did you force the door?"

Liam's low, steady voice powered Thomas's fury with the bad intel and a mistake he'd never be able to fix—the moment he'd give anything to live a different way.

"Hell happened." He shoved the coffee table with his foot and Liam's self-satisfied smile became a watchful stare. Thomas enjoyed Liam's apprehension. He wanted more of that. More fear, more certainty that Thomas held life and death—too damn much death—in his hands.

"At the top of the stairs," Liam said again.

"No."

"Face it."

"Like I'll ever forget. I face it every second all day and night long." He stood and barely stopped himself from kicking Liam Webster's safe-at-home head. The man had never looked death in the eye. Never been forced to kill. Never sacrificed the lives of people who depended on him because he'd hesitated before he recognized the real enemy. "Forget this. You know nothing and you'll do yourself a favor if you get out of here."

He turned to leave, but Liam startled him, standing up. Thomas waited, a hunter with his eye on prey. Longing for revenge—to make someone pay for all the mistakes. Someone he didn't love like a brother.

Liam recognized the danger. Fight-or-flight had to be running hard in his blood. "You're in bad shape," he said. "You offered me coffee ten minutes ago, and now you want to kill me."

"More than you know."

"Why?"

Thomas shook his head, seeing children at the funerals, a mother and father bereft, wives who'd thanked him for doing his best. *His best.* Those lonely women, never again to be held by the men who'd been his responsibility.

"Why?" Liam raised his voice, testing.

Because I'm out-of-freaking-control. "Someone needs to die."

"Someone?"

Thomas saw himself in the other man's eyes. A phantom. Exactly the kind of soldier he was supposed to be. A man who worked in silence, who took out his hostage or his enemy and left no trace, much less the bodies of friends and innocents.

"Who's supposed to die, Thomas?"

"You know." He gagged. "This game's too easy, and you're too predictable."

"Until you tell me, I won't leave you alone with Abby so you can make her a victim, too."

Thomas closed the few feet between them. Before he knew what he was doing, he had the other man by the throat. "I'd never hurt Abby." Tears burned at his eyes because he didn't know if he was lying. "Never."

"I'm another question, though." Liam actually smiled. Too smart to be afraid. He didn't understand his moments were numbered in single digits as Thomas circled his hand around the tie that could so conveniently act as a noose. "Who was supposed to die, Thomas?"

"Shut up." He let go abruptly, and Liam staggered against the sofa.

Strangling Dr. Webster might end all the pain he could barely stand, but only a weak man chose to die in prison because living was harder.

Liam didn't bother to straighten his clothes. "Unless you throw yourself in front of the next bomb, you will live. You might as well learn to survive, too."

"I threw myself at the bomb, but I wasn't fast enough, and her kids were between us." He saw the woman and the terror in her eyes. "She was a hostage. The cleric's enemies got to him first. They kidnapped the woman and her children. They strapped a bomb to her chest and they hid behind mattresses across the room. When we got the door open, the woman pushed her children at me. She begged me to save them, but I didn't know what she was doing. We saw so many people who were willing…dying to sacrifice…" He cleared his throat, still barely man enough to hold back useless tears. "The children reached for me. I reached for her—"

His stomach rose again. His throat constricted. He threw up on Abby Carlton's living-room floor. But he did not admit he was the one who should have died.

"HERE YOU GO, MRS. MURPHY." Abby passed the ticket she'd just written through the window of a beautiful, classic sports car, careful not to smudge the finish. "If you still think my radar gun is wrong, feel free to meet me in court. Thanks so much for your cooperation."

"Your envy of my car is unattractive, Officer."

The woman shot forward in a plume of gravel and loose dust. Abby considered chasing her down again, but Mrs. Jade Murphy slowed for the next red light and left it at legal speed, so she let her go. Another car pulled in behind Abby's, and she turned.

"Liam?"

He got out, his tie off center, his shirt untucked above his belt buckle. A fight? Good God—please—no. Hadn't she already done enough to him without setting an unstable soldier on him? She searched his face for bruises. His arms and legs worked fine.

"I'm glad I found you," he said.

"Tell me Thomas didn't beat you up."

He scowled. "You assume I'm the loser?"

"You're trained in different areas." She straightened his tie, pretending she wasn't terrified for him. "In a psychology trivia contest, you'll take Thomas every time."

"Don't joke, Abby. You have to be careful in that house. I'm not even sure I should let you stay with him alone."

She let her hands fall to her sides. "You forget I lived with Mom when she used to pray to die."

He looked pained. "Your mother isn't as physically strong as Thomas."

"Don't kid yourself. You've wrestled more than one patient in the middle of a psychotic episode." Panic crawled down her spine as she pictured Liam facing Thomas. "You're sure you're all right?"

He nudged her away, and she remembered she found their friendship more comfortable than he did.

"I'm a man and I could handle him if I had to."

Sweat trickled down the back of her neck. From

fear or the heat of Houston pavement, even under a January sun? "But you two fought?"

"He grabbed me, and then he let me go when I didn't flinch."

"Why do you think he did that?"

"Why do you think, Abby?" It wasn't like Liam to lose his temper. "He's riddled with guilt, and he wants to pay, but no one's willing to kill him. I'm worried he'll find a way to make it worthwhile."

"Survivor's guilt. You just have to teach him to survive, Liam."

"I love a good pep talk. Now listen to me."

"How could I not? You're shouting."

"The traffic's loud."

And curious. Passing drivers peered through their windows at the cop and the irate man on the side of the road.

"Calm down, buddy." She said it with laughter in her voice, but for once, Liam ignored her teasing.

"I feel for the guy, Abby, and I know you can't resist a wounded animal, but his injuries are too traumatic. What if he came at you?"

"He won't." How she knew, she couldn't say. He wasn't a nurturing man, like Liam, but she trusted Thomas.

"He's not the same man you planned to marry."

"He never was," she said. "And we've covered all this." Her relationship with Thomas had been part of the debris of her and Liam's marriage. "I'm not the same woman he knew, either."

"He could shake you like a rag doll."

"He won't. I'm sorry if he scared you—"

"He didn't scare me."

Men. "I'm sorry for whatever he did, but I'm not afraid of him. Besides, if he loses it, I have contacts with the police department. When I call, someone comes."

Liam frowned as if he'd like to shake her himself. "This is what makes me crazy about you and Thomas Riley. Why does he always come first with you?"

"First? I don't know what you're talking about." She tried to move him back toward his car, but he resisted. "He's like Janie to me."

"That homeless woman you've made your new best friend?"

"I'm not a big fan of sarcasm."

"Neither am I." At last he straightened his shirt. "And I understand about Janie and her problems, but you never gave her a room in your house."

He'd had no reason to know she'd let Janie use her spare room once or twice. "I'm not one of your patients." As their marriage began to fail, he'd tried to analyze her—most annoying. Divorce had given them a strong friendship she didn't intend to ruin.

Liam headed back to his car at last, and she trotted to keep up. "You never listen to me," he said.

"I listen. I just don't want to admit it." She rubbed his rumpled shirtsleeve. "I like to manage my own life."

With one arm, he yanked her close. "I wish I didn't feel this compulsion to take care of you, Abby. You're a walking target." He kissed the top of her head. "You care too much."

"You're one to talk. How many guys are generous enough to treat an ex-wife's ex?"

"We're both a couple of bleeding hearts. Do me one favor."

"Okay." She waved a slowing car on by.

"Keep your cell phone at your side, and hit 911 the second you're worried."

He thought she'd need to? She hid her shock. "Deal. If you'll answer a question I'm not allowed to ask." He looked confused, and she wished she didn't have to break his patient confidentiality with Thomas, but she'd lived through a lot of scary nights with her mother, and she had to know what she might face at home. "Do you think he could hurt himself in my guest room?"

"You mean kill himself? No. He'd consider suicide running away, and he wouldn't want you to find him. He already thinks he's let down enough people who believed in him." Liam reached for his car door. "Be careful. Okay?"

"I always am. You don't want to share the name of the cop who told you where to find me?"

He laughed over his shoulder. "Sorry. Confidential."

The second he turned out of sight, she consulted her watch. Several hours before she went off duty. She returned to her own car and called home. No answer. Her house was too far out of her sector for a drive-by.

Instead of putting her on her guard, Liam's visit had made her more worried about Thomas. Liam didn't spook easy, and he'd obviously been concerned that she'd walk into a disaster when she went home.

She considered calling one of the patrolmen who handled her neighborhood, but Thomas and a stranger might be a bad mix. Abby stared at the passing traffic, the bright winter sun off to the east, a ragged strand of leftover Christmas garland twisting off a street lamp in the breeze.

She'd taken a lot of shifts for fellow officers with crises at home. Time to call in a favor. Even if Thomas shot her as she opened the no-doubt-securely-dead-bolted front door, she had to make sure he was all right.

CHAPTER FIVE

WITH KEYS IN ONE HAND, her uniform in the other and a bag of groceries over her wrist, Abby wrestled her door open. Her shopping and uniform were props to make her look normal, not frantic, showing up early. She draped her uniform over the banister, dropped her keys on the stair tread and looked for Thomas in the living room.

He got up from the sofa, tall and tense and unfamiliar, moving with the stealth of a predator.

"Hey," she said.

He stared at her with empty eyes. He was still in the place Liam had taken him.

"Do you want to talk?"

He turned toward the stairs, his expression unchanged. "I can't think of a worse idea, Abby."

She hardly recognized his voice, and it unnerved her. Leery of leaving him alone no matter what Liam had said, she held up her grocery bag. "How about lunch?"

"Not hungry. Thanks." His clipped tones vibrated,

and she knew his concern was for her. He didn't trust himself.

Abby stepped back. Their unfinished past made her forget she'd already left him once. She couldn't stand seeing him in so much pain.

He continued up the stairs, so stiff his legs seemed to jerk him along. She clung to the banister and kept her mouth shut.

Every instinct and all her training prompted her to go up there and find some way to help Thomas, but he'd asked her to leave him alone. Same old story. She wanted to be part of his life, and he considered himself better off without her. He even considered her better off without him.

Abby started a more elaborate lunch than she usually cooked for herself, hoping aromas of baking chicken and herbed potatoes might drag Thomas downstairs. They didn't.

She waited while the food cooled. At last, she choked down a couple of bites to persuade herself she hadn't cooked only for him. Then she cleared the table, cleaned the kitchen and sifted through the magazines on the living-room coffee table without absorbing a single word.

At just before six, she made a ham-and-cheese sandwich and poured a glass of milk. She climbed the stairs without letting herself think of what she might find behind Thomas's door.

He didn't answer her knock. Not the first or the

second. Finally, instead of hitting the door with the sandwich plate a third time, she balanced it on her elbow and turned the doorknob. He hadn't locked her out.

She would have if she'd wanted to be alone. Maybe Liam was right and Thomas needed comfort, but didn't know how to ask. She eased the door open.

Darkness smothered his room. He'd shut the drapes and blinds.

"Thomas?" When he still didn't answer, fear grabbed her by the throat. "Thomas." She dumped the plate and glass on the dresser and hurried to the bedside to reach for the lamp switch.

A hand covered her wrist. "You can open the curtains, but don't turn that on."

He let her go and she crossed to the window. Dusky winter light poured through the glass panes, exposing Thomas, ramrod straight, in an armchair beside the bed.

"What are you thinking?" Danger filled his stillness and the room. "I'm sorry. That's none of my business. I couldn't take the silence up here."

He didn't speak.

"Obviously, you're not hungry, but you have to eat." She went back to the dresser.

"No." Reaching her side before she knew he'd moved, he took her hand again. "I can't keep food down when I'm like this. Let it go."

Thomas had never allowed her to see him this

way before. "I don't know how to help. Should I call Liam back?"

"No." He made her jump. Not just because of his raised voice. Nothing had ever frightened him before, but she would have said he was afraid to talk to Liam.

"Then talk to me. I don't want you to any more than you want to try. I'm afraid to hear what's made you so upset, but maybe talking would help."

"Can't you see that saying it out loud only made it worse?" His breath brushed her forehead. Heat surged and pooled around them. She tried not to inhale his scent, familiar and disturbing at the same time.

Something was wrong. She knew how to handle a man in trouble, but Thomas wasn't like the distressed people she helped care for on the job.

Thomas had answered enough of Liam's questions to open all his injuries. Finally, she understood his lack of concern for the shrapnel. Physical pain must seem like a relief compared to the torture of his guilt.

Liam had warned her. She should have listened. But someone had to help Thomas escape his demons. They were fastened to his back so tightly she could almost touch them.

"Thomas."

He turned only his head, but walked to the door. "I came up here to keep you out of my reach." Huskiness blunted his tone. "I'm not trying to be rude, but you should go."

"You'd never hurt a woman. Why should I go?" she asked. "I'm your friend."

"You and I will never be friends." He inhaled, his shoulders rising. "I don't want to scare you, but my head is full of—" Lifting both hands to his temples, he ground his palms into his eyes as if he were trying to erase the pictures he saw.

"Can't you let me…" Words wouldn't come. Six years ago, she would have opened her arms and offered him whatever he needed in order to forget.

But maybe that was a good place to start.

Going to him, she brushed her hands across his shoulders first in case those demons really were perched there. His muscles tensed to snapping point. She slid her hands down his back, around his waist, linking them over the waistband of his jeans. Without clear thought, she pressed as close as she could get, resting her cheek on his back.

"You're not alone. I still believe in you."

His overheated skin warmed her face through his cotton T-shirt. Her own heart beat against the back of her throat as she relearned the hard contours of his body.

Unfinished business whispered in her head. She'd left him six years ago, but she'd longed for him. Holding him felt right and wrong all at once. Terrifying need made her stroke the flat plane of his belly. She didn't even pretend her motives were pure.

Thomas wrenched her hands off him.

"Abby." Her name, whispered in a cry for help. She assumed he was pushing her away, but instead, he turned in her arms and linked her hands again behind his back.

He was aroused. She gasped at her instinctive, answering need. He caught her face in his hands, but she was looking at a stranger. She could have reminded him they weren't lovers anymore. She told herself to pull away.

But he closed his eyes and whispered her name again, and the Thomas she'd once loved took the stranger's place. He covered her mouth with his.

Six years—the lack of a decent goodbye—sheer physical yearning. All the logical excuses flitted through her mind as Thomas's mouth incited a desire beyond her control.

With his hands at her waist, he pushed her toward the wall, and she met it with a grunt. She curved her hands over his taut buttocks, seeking only to be closer—closer still.

Thomas found the hem of her T-shirt and pushed it up. He did the same with her bra, not bothering to remove it before he closed his lips over her nipple.

She groaned, threading her fingers through his hair, and Thomas flexed his hands against her skin, making her painfully aware of her own body. She almost knew how she felt to him.

He opened his mouth. Cool air and his moist tongue chilled her breast.

"Thomas." She couldn't help begging.

With a half groan, he stroked her again and again, pausing only to find her other nipple. She shuddered, his to control. She couldn't stop herself. She wanted him, always had, too much.

He stepped back, staring as he yanked his shirt over his head and opened the button at his waistband. The sound of his lowering zipper broke the tense silence. She tried to remember the word *stop,* but she was also afraid it would slip out of her mouth.

His jeans dropped to the floor and he waited for her. This was basic need, not seduction. She took off her own shirt, but struggled with her bra. Thomas muttered something deep in his throat and tore off the bra without hurting her.

"The bed," she said.

He didn't seem to hear. He slid down her body, his mouth hot, hungry, open on her skin as he undid the button and zipper on her jeans and pulled them, along with her panties, down her legs.

Desire welled, sharp, not so terribly joyful. Frightening.

She held on to the wall as Thomas pressed his mouth to her thigh. She nearly sank, but he kept her upright. He tugged her clothing over first one foot and then the other. As she arched against him, he linked his arms around her hips.

"Thomas." She cupped his face. He'd gone too far away. He stood and somehow his boxers were gone, too. Caution reappeared. "We should remember," she began, but lost track of the thought as he took her mouth in another kiss that destroyed her common sense.

"I'm sick with remembering. Help me forget."

He lifted her, pulling her legs around his hips as he kissed her over and over again. Abby searched for some hint that what they were doing was wrong. None came. He'd been her first real love, the man whose memory had ruined a marriage she'd truly wanted.

If Thomas needed her only for tonight, tonight was right. He had claims on her that she didn't understand, but she still couldn't say no. She could only curve her body to help him reach her, ready and hungry and all too willing.

"You're too tall," she said.

He lifted her higher and she linked her arms around his shoulders. Opening his mouth wide against her throat, he entered her with a groan of satisfaction.

The wall was hard, and so were Thomas's demands. She could only respond, offering everything he wanted, down to a sampling of her soul. It had belonged to him anyway once upon a time.

Pleasure, unbelievable and intense, uncoiled inside her. A depth of pleasure she'd never known even with Thomas.

She tightened her arms, focused only on him, his breath mingling with hers, his voice whispering pieces of words in her mouth. The intimacy of love made in despair.

His breathing sharpened. His rhythm faltered and he flattened his hands against the wall. "I can't—" he said against her lips. "I—"

She knew his body too well to misunderstand his incoherent attempt at an apology. "It doesn't matter."

He shuddered as he spilled inside her. With each pulse, her body quivered. Gasping, he turned his face away, but she kissed his cheek, his chin, tasting sweat and salt.

Only as she clung, feeling the tremors of his release, did she remember they hadn't used protection.

HIS KNEES THREATENED to lock. Far too late, he tried not to hurt Abby as he braced her body between his own and the wall. He'd been too rough. He'd lost all control.

"Are you all right?" She'd be bruised from her head to the small of her back. Wrapped around him because he'd been too demanding to find the bed he vaguely remembered her asking for. Straightening, he turned and carried her to it, hardly strong enough to hold her any longer as he lowered her onto the comforter.

He'd taken her selfishly.

Still, she curled against him as if she needed his body heat. Her nipples, hard with excitement, scraped his chest. Her mouth, soft and comforting, sought his. Astounded, he felt an emotion that reminded him of joy.

How did a man thank a woman for reminding him he still lived?

He slid down her body, tasting her, from her throat to the soft full breasts that filled his hands, the tips that teased his tongue. She shifted beneath him, her hips arching.

Curving his mouth in a smile of ridiculous relief, he followed her breastbone. She opened her legs and he wrapped an arm around one of her thighs, but suddenly, she stiffened.

"Wait," she said.

"Not my strong point tonight." He pushed up, searching her face in the scarce moonlight. He wouldn't blame her for stopping him now. "Second thoughts?"

"Sort of." She met his gaze, her eyes filled with trust he didn't deserve. "But not because of you." She eased out from under him, and he felt empty without her in his arms. "I'll be back," she said.

He rolled to his side as she hurried from the room, her body a shadow of pale curves. Staring at the darkness, deeper outside his open door, he listened while she searched through drawers in another room. Her room.

When she came back, she climbed across him, dropping a square package on the bed. He stared at it as the truth dawned.

"You're not using birth control?"

She shook her head. "I forgot. It sounds crazy, but nothing like that ever happened before."

His only thought had been finding peace in her body. "To me, either."

"Let's not talk about it." She seemed to think he meant the quick, rough sex, but he meant that he'd had to have her—would have pleaded with her if she hadn't been willing. Abby's gaze, flat and fierce, rejected any hint of an argument. "We can't change it now and maybe we'll be all right."

"Neither of us lives our lives on 'maybe's.'" He tried to hold her closer, but she straddled his hips. She wouldn't let him put his arms around her so he cupped his hand under her chin. "I'm sorry, Abby."

She hung above him for a moment, unmoving. "I'm just as much at fault." She sank onto him, pushing her hands beneath his back to hold him. Her breasts flattened against his chest. She slipped her legs around his, her touch almost too sensual to bear.

Long denied, his body had no conscience. He found the curve of her spine with his fingers, relishing her shiver. Abby's back was an erogenous zone he'd always explored with fascination. She raised herself again, and he tried to see what she was thinking—but her hair covered her soft cheeks and her eyes slid shut.

He reached for the package. She was a secret and a mystery. And she was precious to him.

ABBY WOKE WITH Thomas's face cradled in the curve of her neck, his breath warming her left shoulder. She wriggled out of his arms, slid off the bed and eased out of the room, sighing with relief when she managed to shut the door before he moved. Abandoning him without good-morning conversation was safer than facing the night she'd just spent in his arms.

Talk about second thoughts. She was smarter than she'd been last night. Too smart to give herself to a man and a past she couldn't afford to repeat.

She showered in her bathroom and dressed in jeans and a sweater. She paused to listen at Thomas's door on her way downstairs. He might be avoiding her, too, but she hoped he was getting some much-needed rest.

Downstairs, she yanked on her jacket and grabbed her uniform and keys, turning back to set the alarm before she locked the door.

The temperature had fallen this morning. She stumbled to her car, tugging the sides of her jacket closed. At the station, she changed quickly in the locker room and sat through roll call, trying to keep her mind on the announcements, instead of wallowing in confusion that could get her into serious trouble on patrol.

Abby joined the stream of other officers all heading for their cars. The job. She had to keep her mind on the job. She wasn't about to let Thomas distract her from her career again.

Warily, she thought of her friends. She'd be looking for them everywhere today. Sometimes she ran into one or the other as they answered calls, too. Mei and Crista would never keep repeating a career-destroying mistake. Could it be a coincidence that with their six-woman friendship broken, she was whirling through her own life with the destructive force of a cyclone?

A guy speeding through a school zone received the short end of her tongue and the long sweep of her pen on his ticket. She felt no guilt for taking her frustration out on him. A responsible guy didn't speed through school zones.

Nor did a responsible woman make love with a former fiancé, and then just keep making love all night long. That first time—maybe that was understandable. His pain had been an open well, and she'd felt an imperative need to comfort him. But the rest of the night? She had no defense.

As she rejoined the flow of traffic, her cell phone rang. She checked the caller ID, expecting to see her own home number. Instead, it was Liam.

She considered ignoring it. But somehow, he'd know she'd turned into a perverse Florence Nightingale and would keep calling if she didn't answer.

Remorse drenched her hello.

"Abby?" He already sounded concerned. "What's wrong?"

"I'm out of breath. Just finished a call."

"You're all right?"

"Sure. Some guy with a lead foot didn't want his ticket. What's up with you?"

"Obviously, I'm checking on you," he said. "You and Thomas were okay last night?"

"Fine." She didn't trust herself with more than a single word. Liam was too good at his job to be fooled for long.

"No problems when you got home?"

Disasters. But they might avoid long-term problems if she remembered she was a mature, adult woman. "We were fine. Thomas stayed in his room." Though she hadn't told an actual lie, she flinched as heat scalded her skin.

"Good. I'm on my way to your house now. Maybe he'll be over the worst shock from yesterday's session."

"I hope so. I could tell it was difficult for him." Especially if he'd talked the way he'd made love, without restraint. "Will you call me after you finish?"

"I can't spill my guts every time I talk to him. That's why the two of you chose me, remember?"

"You could let me know how he's feeling."

"I like your new maternal tone."

Maternal? She hoped not.

Memories of the night before went through her mind. She had to swallow a groan as echoes of passion unexpectedly swept through her. "Yeah."

"I'll call you, but don't worry. I am as good as you and Thomas hope. We'll have him out of your house before you know it."

Thank God. He couldn't leave soon enough. "Good."

"I'm glad we agree for once."

Abby dropped her cell phone on the passenger seat. As she rolled around the next corner, she spied her friend, Janie, exiting a grocer's with the careful step of the inebriated. In a dark blue parka with duct tape over a tear in the shoulder, layered over two pink sweaters, Janie looked almost too warm, unless she'd been on the streets all night.

Abby pulled to the curb. Janie had won her battle with vodka for the past two months, but it hadn't been her longest triumph. Abby put down her window and leaned across, grimacing as cold wind hit her face.

"What are you doing, Janie?"

"Trying to stay warm." The other woman fingered long gray curls over her shoulder. "Gotta get more shelter beds in this town, Officer Carlton."

"I know." Alcohol fumes floated into the car on

Janie's breath. Red lines striated the whites of her pale blue eyes. Abby glanced beyond her at the clouds beginning to form in the high, flat sky. It was even colder than when she'd left home. She opened her door and got out. Trying to see if Janie was carrying a replenished stock of vodka in her plastic shopping bag, she walked around to open the back passenger door. "Why don't we start hunting for your bed early today?"

"No one will take me in yet."

"You forget I have connections." Sad connections, but at least she knew how to keep someone safe. "Why didn't you call me instead of your favorite brand last night?"

"Maybe I did come by your house." She said it as she slid into the back seat.

It was an odd thing for her to say. Abby stopped, but immediately forced herself into motion. Janie would have rung the doorbell.

But would she or Thomas have heard it?

She got in the driver's seat again and started the car. "Did you drop by?"

Janie shook her head without meeting Abby's gaze in the rearview mirror. "I didn't even have money for a phone call, much less bus fare. And how long has it been since I could walk that far in the cold?"

"Where'd you sleep?"

"Who slept?"

Abby took her hint and dropped the subject. "I think we'll try Reverend Michael's shelter first."

"Because of the AA meetings they run there?"

"Every hour on the hour." They'd never bothered to be gentle with each others' feelings, and she refused to pretend the bottle really made Janie's life more bearable.

"I don't have to attend a meeting if I take a bed, you know."

"Right, but you'd feel better if you made meetings every day."

"This weather makes me disagreeable enough to stay away from meetings just because I'm mad."

"Your choice, but bad weather should make you more careful. You could freeze to death on the streets."

"Not in Houston. I'm just glad a storm's coming. That freakin' sun gave me a miserable headache."

It wasn't a great excuse, but Abby's own judgment was so bad she had no room to preach. "We're almost there."

She spent the next hour negotiating with Reverend Michael to commit a bed to Janie before the evening rush. Janie indulged in a tantrum the likes of which Abby hadn't seen since she'd first met the woman. After a night on the street, Janie felt she deserved a bed.

Abby tried to calm her and meanwhile kept at the minister until they settled on terms. Janie agreed to attend an AA meeting, help with a little cleaning and serve the evening meal.

"Just like a job." Her brittle voice cut like glass. Abby rubbed the knots in the back of her neck. If Janie learned to resist drink, she might move on to finding a real job.

"I have to go," she said as Janie draped her threadbare sweater over the end of the metal cot she'd occupy tonight. "Try to make the best of today." She usually avoided lame advice her friend would ignore anyway, but Janie seemed to fall off the wagon more than she stayed on these days.

"I'll walk you out, Abby." Reverend Michael led her down the long aisle between beds in the converted school gym. Once the local independent school district had condemned this building, the minister and his group had taken it over and remade it into a shelter that took almost all their money to keep up.

"Hold on a sec." She hurried ahead of him to drop a few dollars in the donation box. Then she waited, adjusting her hat to shield her eyes as she held the door. The minister stopped outside and drew her to a halt beside him in the loose gravel lot.

"I gave in today, but you know we can't do this often. It wouldn't be fair to the others." The others were the cold and hungry who'd stream in with the darkening sky of evening.

"Janie's fragile today or I wouldn't have asked."

"Because she's been drinking." He spoke with despair, not disapproval. "I wish we could do more to keep her sober, but Janie's not our only regular client," he said. "And you're not the only cop who drops by here to make me feel I'm to blame when I can't take someone in."

She smiled, rueful because she believed his plight. "I always leave a donation."

"You'd need to win the lottery." He turned back to the door. "I want to help everyone I see, too, Abby, but sometimes you can't do anything more."

He went inside, but turned before he shut the door, with a look that asked her to keep real life in perspective.

Abby went back to her squad car, but the walk felt longer and harder than when she'd gone inside.

Time to think brought last night spinning through her head. The possibility of a pregnancy put her mistake in troubling perspective. She whispered a desperate hope that it wouldn't happen—like an ignorant child. She glanced back at Reverend Michael's closed door. She wasn't so very different from anyone in there.

That knowledge usually kept her working hard. Today it made her sad. She should have learned her lesson six years ago.

CHAPTER SIX

ABBY HAD BARELY PUT HERSELF in service again when dispatch radioed a call for a domestic disturbance, a husband verbally abusing his wife. Abby recognized the address and called to affirm she was en route. She noted her case report number and the time. Officers Craig and Durham called that they'd back her up.

They arrived at the Lender house at almost the same minute. Abby parked first and strode up the walkway with the other two officers behind her.

"I've been here several times," she said to Dennis Craig. "The wife always refuses to prosecute."

"They said it was verbal." He had a hand on his holstered gun just the same.

"This time," Abby said. She nodded to Fran Durham. "I'll go first. Just keep an eye open."

She rang the bell, and Bella Lender opened the door, her hair mussed, her eyes red from crying. "Officer Carlton." She burst into tears.

"May we come in?" Abby was already searching the wide living room over the woman's shoulders.

From the far corner, on a clean, but threadbare rug, Bart Lender faced them all.

Abby shuddered. She recognized the look in his eyes. Thomas had stared at her with exactly that soulless expression after he'd talked with Liam.

"Mr. Lender?"

"I didn't start it." He looked around, flexing his hands as if he was searching for something to break in the small, spotless room.

For the first time since she'd joined the CIT, Abby wondered if she was the right officer to field this call. Lender had a reputation for being plain mean, but Thomas's experience made her question why this man might be driven to torture his family. She shook her head. Nothing excused the way he treated his wife and sons.

"Mrs. Lender, may we come in?" she asked again.

Bella stood aside, her body slightly stooped, as if she was ready to take cover at any moment. Abby moved closer to her.

"Are you hurt?"

"No." Straightening, she clutched one arm with the other hand.

Abby nodded, but she held in a sigh. This was going like every other visit she'd made to the home. "Mr. Lender, how would you like to leave for tonight? Maybe talk things over with a counselor tomorrow? I can set you up with a family therapist."

"I said it's not my fault." He came out of the corner.

Durham and Craig met him, putting themselves between the angry man and his wife, whom Abby shifted behind her.

He stopped. "It's not my fault." He lowered his voice, not challenging their greater strength.

Abby tried with his wife again. "How about taking the children somewhere else tonight, Bella? I'll find you a nice place."

"No." She risked a glance at her husband, though Abby tried to block him from her view. Last time she'd taken her two young sons to a women's shelter, Mr. Lender had beaten her as a welcome home.

"Come on, Bella. Can't you see you're headed for disaster?"

"You don't understand. My boys love their father. In his way, Bart loves them—loves us." She wavered and stopped.

"You can't even convince yourself anymore, and I've been here too many times to believe you can fix this without outside help."

"Stay out of my family's business, bitch."

Abby rounded on the man, keeping his wife's position foremost in her mind. "I think you should take a break from the house, Mr. Lender. You've disturbed the peace. We can ticket you for that. You've all but threatened me. If you go any further, I will charge you for that. I'm trying to help your family."

"You don't know about us. You're some gal in a

fancy uniform who likes to push people around. Well, the gun lets you, but take that gun off—"

"That's it." Fran Durham bent the man's arm behind his back, and when he began to struggle, Craig took the other. "Let's step outside, Mr. Lender. You could use some cool air."

He passed Abby with a malevolent stare. She moved with him, keeping his wife out of his reach. When she turned around Bella looked exhausted.

"Consider a shelter, Bella."

"He's right about one thing. You don't understand why he's like this. His own dad kicked him around. He was a small kid at school. He got on the bad side of a gang. And every job he gets, something goes wrong."

How could she still love him? "I can't believe you buy those excuses. Maybe they were good reasons for his behavior when he was sixteen, but he's a man now, with a man's responsibilities. He has to learn to treat you right before you or the boys get hurt. You don't want that."

"He's my husband. I can't even afford the utilities to live here without his paycheck."

"Can you afford to let your sons use him as an example?" Abby glanced toward the hall. "Where are they? Locked in their room again?"

"They know what to do."

Abby wanted to shout at Bella. Why didn't their "knowing what to do" horrify the woman? "This isn't good enough for them. Please, come with me tonight. Stay a couple of days at the women's center and see what happens with Bart. Maybe if he realizes you won't live like this he'll agree to therapy."

"And maybe the second you leave I'll get a broken arm."

"If he touches you again, I'm taking him in, Bella. I'll make sure someone is here often enough to hear the first peep out of him."

Bella flinched. Now that, she seemed to see as a real threat. "Maybe I don't want you to interfere, either, Officer Carlton."

"Too late. If you won't let me help you, I'll help the boys because I don't want to visit their houses in my golden years, trying to talk their wives into escaping a violent home."

"My boys would never—"

"You don't know what your boys will do if you let them believe a good man beats up his wife and children. What if they get a little older and start hitting you, too? Forget about how you'd feel. How will they feel if one day, you argue with them and they take a swing at you? Because that's what their daddy does."

"I can't take any more." Bella dropped onto the sofa to bury her face in her hands. "First him, now you. Why does everyone yell at me all the time? Why can't anyone leave me alone?"

Abby took a deep breath. She was off her game

after seeing something of Thomas in Bart Lender's eyes. "I'm not blaming you for any of this, Bella, but think of the boys."

"I want some peace. One quiet day where no one shouts at me and no one wants anything. Can't you see how much I need that?"

Sitting, Abby wrapped her arm around the other woman's slight shoulders. "I guess your sons could use one of those days, too. Maybe even Bart. That's why I think you should try a break from each other until you work out a truce."

"I love him, officer."

"I know."

Bella sobbed, and Abby held her while she shook. Down the hall, a door opened. Abby willed the boys to stay in their room. They shouldn't see their mother in this shape. They shouldn't be forced to be the men in her life, to comfort her because of the havoc their father caused.

Apparently, Bella crying was a signal to stay put because the door shut again, and no footsteps sounded in the hall.

Abby sat up straighter. "No one else is here?"

"No. They won't come out while I'm crying. That's the rule. I can never be sure crying won't make Bart—" This time, Bella seemed to hear her own words. "Okay," she said. "For tonight. Will you help me pack? And will those other officers keep Bart outside while the boys and I get ready?"

"Sure. I'll drive you to the shelter myself."

"Thanks." Bella looked up. Tears floated out of the corners of her eyes. "But what if he's worse when we come home?"

"What if he's worse if we leave you here with him? You can't be sure of anything except what you want. Maybe you should consider staying away until you know you'll be safe."

Bella looked up, an old woman peering out of her eyes, and Abby ached for her. She obviously believed she might never be safe again.

"While you're packing, I want to talk to Officer Craig. Okay?"

Bella nodded. Abby waited until she'd gone into the boys' bedroom before she opened the front door. Lender was leaning against Craig's car, puffing on a cigarette. They all looked up as Abby came out. She motioned for Craig to come over.

He met her just outside the doorway.

"I'm taking Mrs. Lender and the boys to a shelter. Dennis, do you think you can reach this man at all?"

"I don't know. He's a little calmer, but it won't take much to light his fuse again."

"We have to do something." She glanced back. "She seems to love him, and she wants to stay with him."

"I don't get it."

She shrugged. "Me, either, frankly, but maybe

something sets him off. Did he tell you what made him so angry today?"

"He got fired. The thing is, he probably deserved it. You know this guy. We can't make him change just because his wife and kids would have an easier life if he did."

"Could you say that to him?"

Craig tilted his cap back, reluctance plain. "What's the point?"

"I'd give it a try myself, but he blames me for what's happening."

"You're not kidding." Craig twisted his mouth. "All right. I'll give it a try, but I wouldn't bet on a long-term result. Just get the family out of here, and I'll try to impress upon him that he doesn't need to use his wife as a punching bag."

Abby sharpened her gaze. "Impress upon him?"

Craig's scowl reminded her she wasn't the only person sworn to protect and defend. "You know I don't use force."

"Sorry." Abby gripped his wrist in an apology. "I'm having a hard week."

"And you're about to have a worse day. Doing the paperwork from this will take you until the end of shift."

"Yeah, I'd better get going."

He was right, but after they got past Bart Lender without mishap, the rest looked like running downhill. The boys waved goodbye to their dad from the back of Abby's car, and he actually waved back at them.

"He's not a bad man," Bella said.

A wave didn't alter Abby's impression. In case Bella was trying to convince herself, Abby kept her opinion private.

THOMAS BOUGHT TAKEOUT for dinner. Abby's favorite vegetable stir-fry and a spicy chicken dish for himself. He warmed it in the oven and started watching the clock just after four.

Maybe Liam had called her after their session this morning and warned her to stay away. After promising to be honest with his unwilling therapist, Thomas had found he couldn't admit what had happened between himself and Abby. Liam's first question had been about her—how had things gone last night? Thomas understood the other man was only concerned, but he'd stalled through the rest of the session Liam had finally cut short in disgust.

Afterward Thomas had run for an hour, come home for a shower and then wandered the house until he'd run for another hour to shut down the guilty nagging in his mind.

Finally, he decided to get dinner in return for part of his keep around here. Dinner, which might just be desiccated by the time Abby came home.

The phone rang. He found the receiver on a table beside the living-room window and said hello.

"It's Liam."

"Did you call to quit?"

"I thought I'd ask if you wanted to. I've had to re-arrange my schedule to fit in your sessions, but if you don't want to use the time, I have other patients."

He didn't like being threatened, but Liam was right. He'd be an idiot to waste the man's time, and he had to find a way back to his place in his own life.

"I'm sorry about today," he said. "I'll be ready tomorrow."

"To work?"

"Yes."

"Good. Is Abby home yet?"

"No."

"Tell her I called."

"Okay."

And that was it. Liam took his word, which heaped a load of shame onto Thomas's shoulders.

He turned off the phone and set it back on the table just as Abby parked two houses down the street. She got out of the car, sparing a careful glance at her home. Then she reached in the back seat for her uniform.

Thomas opened the door for her. She stared at him, neither smiling nor frowning as she climbed the porch steps.

"We need to talk," she said.

"I know. You don't have to offer any trite reasons to let me down easy. We already spent a lot of time figuring out I don't do the wife-and-kiddies life. Last night we made a mistake, which we won't repeat."

She passed him, her jaw set, and he shut the door. "You covered it all," she said. "I guess I don't have to say anything." She dropped her keys on the stair tread and sniffed the air. "Do I smell a peace offering in the kitchen?"

He smiled. "Last night was my fault, Abby. You don't have to be this upset."

She draped her uniform over the banister. Weariness flattened her expression. She wouldn't burst into song this evening. "Does Liam know you look for a lion's share of guilt?"

Liam was at least as smart as she gave him credit for. "I think he has an idea." Thomas pointed down the hall. "Hungry?"

"Starving. I had a long call this afternoon and missed lunch."

"Let's go then."

She was already on her way. He tried not to watch her walk, couldn't help imagining her graceful body, nude as she'd been last night. He hurried to get ahead of her.

"Liam called." He glanced over his shoulder, pathetically, to see what she felt at the mention of her ex-husband's name.

She hardly showed any response. "Did he ask me to call back?"

"He didn't say."

She lifted both eyebrows. "Oh." And she turned to the cupboard to take down plates. "I guess he'll call if he wants to talk."

"You're exhausted, Abby. Sit down and let me set the table. Consider it my community service."

"Do you ever set it at home?"

Her question surprised him. "What do you really want to know?"

"You always complained I fussed over the table."

She couldn't guess how he'd missed those cozy dinners. "I'm not used to a woman's touch around the house."

"You're still not?"

"No. I already told you that."

She blushed, and he wished he'd been gentler. "I'm feeling grungy," she said. "Maybe I'll wash up before we eat."

He opened the oven door. "Hurry. This stuff's been warming for at least an hour."

"Sorry." She paused at the hallway. "I had to drop someone off at a shelter, and then writing the reports took forever."

"You don't have to explain."

"Right, I don't. We don't want to fall into old habits." She pushed her hair away from her face.

"I'm not confused about last night, Abby." Nevertheless, her remark cut like a knife.

"I didn't mean that. I saw a guy today who wasn't

treating his wife well. I've been to that house several times." She flexed her fingertips against her temples. "But I've always been angry before—that he could hurt her. Today, I saw something in his eyes that reminded me of you since you've come back. I thought he might have a reason for the things he was doing."

He flinched. "Am I that messed up, Abby? You think I'd hurt someone? Someone weaker than I am—someone who loved me? I assume she loves him, or she wouldn't stay?"

"Honestly, I don't understand that kind of love, but no," she said, sounding more convinced as she went. "No, or you wouldn't be here, getting help."

He leaned against the counter, trying to cover his crushing self-doubt, but he couldn't help gripping the lip of the granite top with all his might. "I can survive, not being sure who I am, but I've been assuming you were right about me."

She looked uncertain.

"When you said you believed in me, I listened." He gripped even harder. "I slide to the end of my rope, and then I hang on to your faith."

Her smile offered warmth she'd give any victim who needed her. "I do believe, but I'd better not forget you don't need me long-term."

"What?" A scowl reflected his confusion.

"I can't afford to let you come between me and my work."

His pulse jerked into high gear. They'd broached a forbidden topic. "That's how I felt six years ago."

"Yes, but I'm capable of separating the two." She slid in the verbal knife as if she had no idea it was lethal. "I'll be back in a minute. A shower sounds pretty good."

He couldn't move after she left. He wanted her now as much as he had last night. Six years had dropped away like one vast lonely day, but she assumed he hadn't changed.

He set the table as if they'd never stopped playing house, but Abby was right, and he couldn't persuade her with empty promises. He wanted her. He'd felt almost normal in her arms last night. But she deserved more than a guy who'd already wrecked her life once, mistakenly thinking he could become a husband.

AT FIRST SHE THOUGHT the ringing phone was a dream. She willed someone to answer it until finally she sat up, staring into the dark, breathing hard.

She jerked the phone off the table and muttered, "Yeah?"

"Abby, sorry to bother you. This is Reverend Michael."

"Huh?"

"You have to come get Janie."

That woke her. She licked her lips and rolled out of bed. "What happened?"

"She managed to stash a bottle of vodka, and she's had most of it." He muffled the phone and turned away, shouting something she couldn't understand. Then he moved his hand again. "I threw away the bottle, and she's wrecking the place. I have to call the cops if you don't come."

She was already yanking her T-shirt over her head. "I'm on my way."

She slammed down the phone and pulled on jeans and an HPD sweatshirt. With one foot in a shoe, she hopped, getting the other one on as she crossed the room. Thomas met her in the hall, putting on a sweater.

"Your mother?" he asked.

She stared at him. His hair on end, his face creased by sleep, he still looked so handsome and familiar he cut off her ability to breathe.

"No." She finally turned toward the stairs. "It's work. Go back to bed."

"I'm coming with you." Leaving her in no doubt, he followed her down the stairs.

"You can't go to work with me."

"You aren't working." He pointed to her clothes as she turned on him. "No uniform. But something's wrong. Unless you're going to Liam, I'm coming with you."

"Liam?" She shook her head and snatched her keys off the stair tread. "Where'd you get an idea like that?"

"I don't know. I keep thinking you couldn't still be close if you didn't love him."

"I don't have time to talk about my ex-husband." She turned off the alarm and then set it again before she unlocked the door. "No time is good to talk about Liam with you."

She tried to shut the door on him, but he caught it and followed her outside. In a fine show of Neanderthal tactics, he took her keys and locked it. "I'll drive."

"No, you won't."

"You're never alert for the first hour you're awake, and you're obviously taking care of an emergency. I won't sleep if I let you leave alone in the middle of the night."

Back when they were engaged his concern would have been normal—well, acceptable. Shivering in a cold night, she assumed his need for control was a problem Liam could help him fix. "I'm different. My job requires me to pay attention. Give me my keys."

He handed them over, but he jogged at her side to the car, and she was grateful he didn't run circles around her.

She unlocked the driver's door and made her final stand. "I'm picking up someone I took to a shelter today. She's not dangerous. You don't need to come."

"If she's in a shelter, why are you picking her up?" He held on to the door so she couldn't shut it. In the moonlight, his eyes glittered. He was far more awake than she. Did his brain ever take a break?

"All right." Might as well tell him. It wasn't his business, but he was costing her time, and Reverend Michael might already have called for other help. "She's causing a problem, and they've thrown her out. I need to go."

"What do you plan to do?"

"Take her somewhere else. Let go of my door."

"Don't start this car." He crossed in front of the hood, his eyes daring her to leave without him.

She might have, but the fight began to look childish. She just didn't want him to meet Janie because he was part of her past, and she'd rather those days didn't leak into her present. It was ridiculous, and too late.

She hit the control that opened all the locks and Thomas got in on the passenger side. She started the engine and dogged the speed limits all the way to Reverend Michael's. Thomas was silent while she dialed through the list of all the shelters she knew. She found a bed for Janie in the second to last place on her speed dial.

"How often does this happen?" Thomas asked as Abby rang the bell at the shelter door.

"You mean Janie? Or anyone?"

"Anyone, I guess. How well do you know this Janie?"

"She's a friend. I've come out for her a couple of times."

"How many of these 'friends' do you have?"

She narrowed her eyes. "You sound like a snob."

"Anyone who cares about you would be concerned that you run this woman from one bad part of town to another in the middle of the night."

"I'm fine." She didn't mention the countless nights she'd worried about him with no way to call and make sure he was all right. "I never let the phone out of reach."

The door opened and Reverend Michael leaned out. "Thank God. You took forever. She's calmer now, but I thought she was going to start a riot." He saw Thomas. "Oh. Hello."

Thomas nodded.

Abby lifted her hand in his direction. "Reverend Michael, this is my friend, Thomas Riley. Thomas, Reverend Michael. He runs this shelter and another one down by the hospital."

The two men shook hands.

"Good to meet you," Thomas said.

"I couldn't be more pleased to see you. Janie's in rare form, and I was worried even Abby might need help handling her."

Thomas frowned at Abby, implying she'd recklessly made light of the situation. He nodded at the other man. "I'm glad to help."

"Come inside."

In the dim glow of night-lights spaced down the narrow hall, the walls in their institutional aqua seemed colder than ever. Abby expected the minister to lead them to the big room that held all the beds.

This shelter couldn't afford cubicles or separate rooms.

Instead, he took them to his office where a tall, broad linebacker-type waited with Janie. The woman immediately stood, her eyes red, her hands quivering. She tucked her sweater around herself with dignity that was painful to witness. Abby wanted to protect her from Thomas's suspicious eyes.

"Janie, take the coat." Reverend Michael lifted a faded, but clean dark green parka from the chair next to Janie's.

"It's not mine."

"So what? Someone donated it. You need a new coat, and this one will keep you warm. Take it." Almost at the limit of his patience, he draped the coat around her shoulders and turned her toward Abby. "Come back when you're feeling better. You were a help to me this afternoon."

Janie turned so fast the coat dropped to the floor. "Was I?" she asked with real wonder.

Abby scooped up the parka, hiding tears that burned her eyes.

"You know you were." The minister patted Janie's shoulder. "You could help someone like me all the time if you'd stop drinking."

"Leave me alone." Janie broke away from him and bumped into Abby.

Thomas moved toward them, but Abby lifted her hand behind Janie's back to stop him.

"You don't understand," Janie said to Reverend Michael.

"Why don't you figure it out and then come explain to me?" the minister said.

Abby took Janie's arm and pulled her toward the door. "We should let these folks get some sleep. I've found another place for you."

Reverend Michael nodded at Abby as she turned back. She shrugged in a silent *I'm sorry.* He waved her off.

Even Janie was quiet as they went down the long hall to the parking lot. Her watchful friend from the office locked the door behind them.

"I don't want to go to another shelter," she said. She jabbed her thumb in Thomas's direction. "Who's this?"

"Thomas Riley. A friend. Thomas, this is Janie Paulsen."

"Hi, Janie." Thomas sounded pretty gentle, considering he'd harassed Abby all the way from home.

She smiled in gratitude, which seemed to embarrass him. She pressed the parka on Janie again.

"Maybe I should stay with you." The other woman fended off the coat once more. She didn't notice Thomas's start of surprise, but Abby couldn't miss it. "I'd hate to wake up anyone else at this hour."

"You can't stay at my place." Abby nodded at Thomas, who looked anything but gentle now. "My friend's staying, and I don't have any more space."

"You have a couch in the living room."

"I'm sorry, Janie." She didn't trust Thomas's hypersensitive reactions with someone as unpredictable as Janie, and the intermingling of her past and present was becoming more uncomfortable by the slow-moving second.

"You're mad at me."

"Not at all." Not entirely true. "I wish you'd stop drinking for good, but I know you don't mean to cause problems."

Janie laughed, bitterness tearing the joy out of it. "Before Reverend Michael said I couldn't come back. I'm glad he changed his mind. You will, too, won't you, Abby?"

"Some other time when my beds aren't all full." Abby tried to smile, but Thomas, smoldering behind Janie's back, distracted her.

Mercifully, the other shelter lay only ten minutes' drive away. Janie insisted Thomas wait in the warm car, gracious now that she'd accepted her fate. Abby walked her into the shelter and saw her settled and promised to look for her in the morning.

Outside again, she burrowed her chin into her sweatshirt collar, dreading the moment she had to open the car door. A movement by the car drew her eye. Thomas waited, leaning against the driver's door.

"Does Liam know you let that woman stay at your house?"

CHAPTER SEVEN

DUMBFOUNDED, ABBY LAUGHED. "That's the best you have? You used to think faster on your feet."

Thomas stared, antagonistic, but a perplexing mixture of relief and anxiety fueled Abby's laughter.

Finally, he smiled, sexy with reluctance. "I'm so pissed I can't manage anything more cogent," he said. "For some reason, you listen to Liam."

"Yeah, I'm not sure why that relationship didn't work out."

"Abby," he said in protest, "I don't want to be such good friends that we discuss the ups and downs of your marriage."

"You don't recognize irony?"

He opened her door. "Get in the car."

"Stop ordering me around, Sergeant Major." But she moved to the door. The cold had her shivering anyway. "I wish you and my parents and Liam would stop smothering me with advice. Despite all your helpful interference, I run my life perfectly well, and I'm happy."

"I see how happy you are." He looked a little mystified. "Inviting homeless women and possibly dangerous men to stay over. You wander the streets of Houston all night. You browbeat shelters to give your charges beds."

"Are you suggesting I throw you out?"

"You probably should." With a dry smile, he shut her door and crossed to the passenger side.

She watched him, uncomfortably aware of his loose-hipped, confident stride. She didn't remark on the progress they'd made since North Carolina where he'd had to drive every time they got in a car together. He'd laughingly suggested it was a "man thing," but Abby had always considered it a "Thomas quirk."

He turned to her as he got in the car. "What would it take to make you listen to me about the chances you're taking?"

"What chances?" She turned the key, glancing at him as the engine started. Because of her mom's illness, she'd been one of the protectors in her family. She began to feel trapped when people, her family and friends, told her she was reckless. "I'm doing my job."

"Your house is an approved shelter?"

"I've known Janie for three years, long enough to trust her."

"I think you want to help Janie because she reminds you of your mother. You don't owe every woman who can't manage her own life."

"I don't confuse Janie with my mom, and you talk big, but tell me you could turn your back on her. I notice you came along."

"Because of you."

"I didn't need you."

"I'm a man. No matter what you think you're capable of doing to protect yourself, I'm stronger than you and stronger than Janie. If something went wrong, a man might be able to handle her. I'm not sure you could."

She eased an impatient breath between her lips. "I've picked up kids on PCP, men who thought they had to prove a female cop 'wasn't the boss of them,' and I've dragged unconscious victims from their burning cars. I'm strong enough to do my job, and I don't go cruising the streets to drum up people who need saving."

"We'll need saving if you don't keep your eyes on the road."

She faced forward and swerved back into her lane. "I'm not trying to make Janie better. I just want to make sure she's safe."

"What about your safety? Janie isn't well."

"You didn't worry about me this much when we were engaged."

"I did." He touched her arm, and her body tensed in an overreaction. "I should have made sure you knew how much you meant to me."

She swallowed, uncertain whether she was about

to cry or warn him this conversation was more dangerous than any decision she'd ever made. "It doesn't matter anymore."

"To you, maybe. I'm still making amends."

"What do you mean?"

"I never committed myself to anyone except you, and then I let you down. You must have hated me. It's the only reason someone as loyal as you would have left. But when I showed up at your door, you never thought twice about helping me. A man's a fool who doesn't appreciate you."

He hadn't littered his speech with hearts and flowers, but she'd wondered for six years how he'd given her up so easily. Despite the gap of time that stretched between them and the fact that he might fall for anyone who trusted him right now, she imagined, for a second, how it would feel to really go home with Thomas tonight.

Then she came to her senses. The Army owned him, and she wasn't good at sharing.

"It's late and we're talking about a time we should leave alone."

"I'll shut up if you promise you'll be on your guard when you go out in the middle of the night for someone like Janie."

"I see a lot of needy people. Maybe they're dangerous, too, but mostly they're sick." She hit her blinker for a right turn. "Don't give me that 'I told you so' look. I'm not trying to cure the people I meet in my job because I can't do that for my mom. You know nothing about Janie."

"Do you?"

Because he asked gently, she told him. "I understand Janie better than Reverend Michael does. Probably better than she does, herself. She didn't always live on the streets."

"How'd she get there?"

"She's looking for her daughter." Abby glanced at him in the dim light of a street lamp. His set face worried her. Maybe he wasn't healthy enough to hear Janie's story. "Are you sure you want to know? It's bad."

"I'm not an invalid." Embarrassment roughened his tone.

"Janie was a high school teacher. Algebra. She lived a nice middle-class life until her sixteen-year-old daughter fell into some trouble. Drinking, and she dabbled in drugs. Janie and her husband tried to help, but the girl fought them. Things got worse until she finally ran away."

"Ran away or disappeared?"

"She left a note. She might have gone with someone, but she left because she wanted to. Janie and her husband spent all their money trying to find her, and then they divorced."

"Just like that?"

"No." Abby had said it without emotion to hide her sadness. How many times had she felt her own mother drifting away, wondered if she might not ever come back?

"Where did they last hear of the girl?"

"Her best friend saw her drop her biology notebook in the trash can on her way out of class, and then she vanished as if the air had swallowed her up. After the divorce, Janie left, too. She moved from town to town, no plan in mind. She'd just arrived in Houston when I met her."

"Why Houston?"

Abby shook her head. "I don't know. She probably doesn't know. It was just the place she ran out of bus fare. I watch her on the street—staring into every face she sees, hoping she'll recognize one of the young women. It's been fifteen years."

"The girl must be dead."

"What mom could live thinking that?"

He turned his head. She felt him looking at her, but the intensity between them kept her from looking back.

"How do you care so much?" His husky voice played her pulse as if she were his instrument.

She'd loved his voice once, smiled every time he said her name. "Why do you care for the things that matter to you?" She glued her eyes to the road, but she needed an answer, for six years ago and for now. How was he able to leave her to fight for nebulous causes in strange lands? Why hadn't she mattered most? He'd come before her job, before her family. Why hadn't he loved her enough to put her first?

"How could I not love my country enough to defend it?" Genuine bemusement deepened his tone. He didn't understand the question. "I don't have to wave a flag or flaunt my uniform. I just love my country."

"How can you be so sure?"

He sighed with his whole body. "I want to be sure. For the first time in my life I'm not."

She glanced at him, but he lifted his head, interpreting quickly.

"Don't misunderstand me," he said. "I should have saved my men and that woman and her kids. I want to go back and not make the same mistake. That's what I want Liam to give me."

"Certainty?" Nausea caught her by surprise. How could Liam give that to anyone?

But Thomas nodded, the movement barely perceptible.

"The kind you had before?"

Again, he nodded. "Yes," he said, as if he needed to hear the word aloud. "Even if you think I was wrong."

"No one's infallible. You understand averages. You were bound to—"

"Fail?"

"I wouldn't call death in a battle failure." What she called it obviously didn't matter. He believed he'd failed. "Liam's only human, you know. He can't make you see something you don't feel."

He didn't answer. Traffic passed them, each car whooshing past with people busy living their own lives. Seconds ticked, slowly, as Abby's palms grew moist gripping the steering wheel.

"Thomas?"

"I don't know." He said it too quickly.

"You scare me."

He laughed, and a shiver ran through her because he clearly saw nothing funny. "How do I scare you?"

"I didn't like worrying about you when you knew you could do no wrong."

He rubbed his temples. "You're not allowed to worry about me anymore."

"Allowed?"

"We're friends, not lovers."

"And friends don't care that much. That's why you came with me tonight? Just bored? Nothing else to do at—" she pointed at the console clock "—3:20 in the morning?"

"Let's drop the subject," he said.

So they wouldn't talk about still being lovers? About how crazy she'd been, leaping over the boundaries of friendship? "That's probably best."

What a relief to turn onto her street. She parked and they crossed to her house. Thomas stood aloof while she entered and handled the alarm.

For once, the familiar scents didn't comfort her. The warm light on her beautiful hardwood floors left her cold. She set the locks and the alarm again, a touch annoyed with her guest. Janie had stayed without stealing any of Abby's sense of being home. Alone with Thomas, she felt unsettled. No man should invade a woman's sanctuary.

She started up the stairs. "Good night." No reason to look back. "I have to get up in about two hours."

"'Night, Abby."

Strain in his voice asked her not to go. She closed her eyes. He couldn't know that gruff note had always seduced her. She loved the way it felt against her ear, inside her head, as his scent wrapped around her. If she walked back down the stairs and wrapped her arms around Thomas, he would not send her away. She could spend the next two hours with him, forgetting work and his job, and the fact that he was leaving again as soon as Liam helped him figure out how to be well.

Abby planted one foot in front of the other until she reached the hall. Then she distracted herself, counting the sixteen steps it took to reach her room. After she closed the door, she turned to stare at the brass knob with its push-button lock. She jabbed the button.

To keep Thomas out? No.

Last night and her unfortunate sexual need for Thomas changed nothing. She just had to remember how alone she'd been when he'd slept beside her in North Carolina.

FRIDAY MORNING Thomas and Liam talked in the kitchen over cups of coffee that grew cold. Their session followed an already familiar routine.

"You still haven't told me what you should have done differently." Safe on the other side of the sun-striped table, Liam could afford to wear that smirk. He always smirked when he repeated his favorite question.

Thomas controlled an increasingly insistent urge to wipe Liam's face clean of all expression. "If I knew, I could tell you to go to hell once and for all." Thomas mopped sweat off his forehead with a napkin.

"You've been over and over those few minutes."

"Yeah—I'm starting to think you like watching people squirm."

Liam shook his head, as if they'd never get anywhere. Thomas wanted to beat the shit out of him.

"I don't mean just with me," Liam said. "It's always in your head. Why relive it if you can't find a better way? How many times have you argued with someone and only thought of a better response later? That's what you're doing. Looking for a better response."

"It wasn't an argument. That woman and her children died and so did three of my best friends. Three men I would have trusted to save me." Thomas stood. "You've never been near a firefight. You're the wrong guy to talk to."

"I wonder why you won't let yourself see a solution."

Thomas saw himself planting his fist in the other man's satisfied face. Every day they covered the same ground, and Liam nagged, as smug as if he'd stacked all the answers in a neat file inside his head.

"Tell me how to fix it. That's why we're here."

"You're the only one who can find the answer. I'll force you to keep thinking until you do."

"I don't have to sit in this room while you act like God once a day just to make me think about that mission."

"You're always angry. Stop wasting your energy and face what you don't want to look at. See the truth."

"Stop shoving platitudes down my throat and say something that helps."

Liam picked up his coffee cup and set it in the sink. Then he came back to the table. "Do your assignments make you angry?"

"At last, a direct question." Thomas sat back and a whiff of baked apples wafted past. This damn kitchen always smelled like home cooking. "I'm never angry during missions. Almost always after, but never during. That's how you get people killed." Liam leaned toward him and Thomas looked square into his memories of that night. "I wasn't angry. Not until I woke up on a hospital ship. I already knew some of my men had to be dead. And those kids…"

"You saw the children die?"

"As much as I saw anything." A flash of light. Blood on white cloth. Baked apples receded before the memory of a sickening coppery scent. Pain as bright and unending as sunlight plunged into his eyes. "I can't tell what I remember from what I imagine."

Suddenly Liam looked over Thomas's shoulder, through the French doors to Abby's garden. He stood.

With his senses working overtime, Thomas rose, too. He looked where Liam was staring. The spreading branch of a spruce waved, when everything else was still. Without thinking, Thomas shoved the civilian behind him.

"What are you doing?" Liam asked. He stepped away, staring harder at the woman who'd moved the limb aside to sniff one of Abby's shrubs. "What's Janie doing here?"

Thomas was more interested in the specifics of her behavior. "Have you ever touched one of those branches? It should hurt." Not only did she seem oblivious to pain, she made no effort to hide. She strolled from tree to tree, examining a bed of pansies, a short, barricade of shrubbery. "You know her?" Thomas couldn't give Abby away. Obviously, Liam didn't know she'd let Janie stay in this house.

"Abby met her on the job. She has some problems." Liam picked up his cell phone and dialed a number. Abby's probably. "Hey," he said after a second. "Do you know how Janie might have discovered where you live?" He waited. Abby's defensive tone, her words unintelligible, came through his phone. Liam turned toward the garden again, frustrated in a way he never was with Thomas. "She's outside in the back. Don't you know it's dangerous to bring her home with you?"

Thomas walked to the door, intent on Janie as he tried not to listen to the conversation behind him.

"I know she's not well, but you're a cop. You're supposed to separate your job from your home life." Another pause. "Okay, okay, but we're going to discuss this. No, I won't bother her, but I'm glad Thomas will be here when you come home."

Thomas tensed. If he were the other man, he couldn't have walked out, depending on anyone else to protect Abby.

Liam hung up. "Can you believe she's had Janie to stay here?"

Thomas wasn't a liar by nature, but he owed Abby. "I'm surprised."

"I have to make her see Janie's not her mother. She's not responsible for Janie's mental health."

Startled that they shared the same theory, Thomas wished him the best of luck. "Abby's stubborn," Thomas said. "But then, I'm lucky she is."

Liam smiled, still forgoing the usual smirk. "Were you angry when you shoved me to safety?"

"Here I was, congratulating you for not being smug, but you had to ruin it."

"Were you angry?"

"No."

"Think about that." Liam took a last anxious look at Janie and turned toward the hall. "We should call the cops, but Abby would kill us if we got Janie arrested for trespassing."

"Or stalking," Thomas said, testing. He might not be the most objective judge.

"I don't think it's that." Liam shoved his phone into his pocket. "But you're making progress. You didn't think twice before you tried to save me."

"Janie's not wearing a bomb. I don't have to order you to walk into certain death or to kill her. You think that wasn't in my head?"

BEFORE SHE PARKED HER CAR, Abby saw Thomas sitting in the uncomfortable wooden rocker on her front porch. If he had a shotgun he'd look fit to terrorize the neighborhood.

She got out, wondering how he could stay so hot about something in such chilly air. She reached in the back for her uniform and then started up the walkway. Thomas rocked, his expression overly serious.

"What happened?" The usual nightmare popped into her head. She searched her windows. Often, when her mom stopped taking her medication, she left Abby's dad and came to roam Abby's house. As if she blamed her husband for her illness. Or maybe she hated letting him see her when she was too sad to take another breath. Either way, most depressive phases started with a trip to Abby's house.

"Mom?" She dropped her hands to her sides. Her uniform dragged on the cement path.

"No." Instantly Thomas hurried down the wooden steps to meet her. "Sorry. I never thought you'd assume the worst."

"What are you doing?" Other than a caveman-protecting-his-own imitation.

"Janie stayed here, wandering around your garden for hours."

"Is she still here?" She peered around the empty yard. "You didn't invite her to stay? That's a bad idea as long as you're here."

Thomas shook his head as if he thought he was hallucinating. "I did not invite her in, and if you ever do again, you're crazy." He opened the front door and waited for her to go inside. "Liam and I were talking in the kitchen this morning when he saw her in the back."

"None of this sounds like Janie. I've never found her hanging around the neighborhood. Why would she do that?"

"We wondered, too."

Abby dumped her things on the stairs as usual. "You're sure she's not back there?" She glanced down the hall to the kitchen, but Thomas shook his head again.

"She left a little over an hour ago. I went out on the front porch to make sure she headed down the street. Maybe she was looking for a bus."

"Thomas, she must have thought you were threatening her."

"I just wanted her to see me if she looked back."

"As a threat," Abby said, annoyed that he'd put on a show to intimidate her friend. "*You* came to *me* for help. I don't need any."

He took her wrist, and she felt small as his large palm surrounded the bone. "Listen to me. You call Janie a friend, but today she was a stalker."

Abby shuddered. Janie's behavior hadn't been normal. "She's not strong enough to stalk. She can't follow the same routine three days in a row." He had to be wrong. She hurried down the hall to the kitchen and then opened the back door to make sure the other woman hadn't come back and hidden from Thomas.

Beneath the porch roof, the shade was cold. She walked into the waning sunlight with Thomas on her heels. Evading him, she lifted a spiky, spruce branch, gasping as a small pointed cone bit her palm.

Thomas pulled her back. "She didn't act hurt when she did that."

"So she's psychotic? Forget it. She's probably lost feeling in her nerve endings from staying in the cold most nights."

"She's not here. If she'd turned back I would have called the police. I don't want her here again."

Abby jerked out of his grasp. "Janie is none of your business. For that matter, neither am I. You made sure of that when you failed to notice I'd left North Carolina."

"I noticed." He licked his lips, but stared at her mouth. Abby tasted him in memory. "I care about you, and I cared back then, but I didn't know how to beg." Need rasped in his voice. "And you were better off."

"Was I?" She reached for him, but memories of the night they'd already spent together stopped her. That night could still bring them disaster.

She wrapped her arms around her own waist, holding back. She ached for him, craved his touch, the slightest pressure of his lips against hers. If only his duty and her need of a full commitment hadn't parted them before. If only either one of them had been strong enough to fight for the other. It was too late now.

"Let me make sure Janie didn't come back." She turned her back on Thomas, unsure she wasn't going to cry at the sight of his bleak face. "I don't know why she'd hang around—"

"Lurk."

"No." Janie's inappropriate behavior troubled her, but Abby couldn't go along with Thomas. "Maybe she wants to know about you. She's possessive because she's already lost someone she loves."

"You're not her possession."

"I don't belong to you, either."

"No." Splaying his fingers on her shoulders, he turned her and then cupped her face in his hands. "But I don't want you hurt. You don't know when to cut someone off."

"Lucky for you." She flung anger in his face because concern—friendship—didn't feel like enough from him.

His hands tightened. "Janie's wrong to come here, and you're irresponsible to think she's normal. You know it. You don't need a psychologist like Liam or a suspicious soldier to make you see."

She shivered as the sun disappeared behind her house's peaked roof and cold fell between them. "You're not here to tell me how to live my life or do my job."

Thomas looked at her as if she'd lost her mind. "So you don't intend to put distance between yourself and Janie? Your superiors wouldn't approve."

"Don't threaten me." Thomas might make sure her bosses found out about Janie if he thought he was keeping her safe.

"Public services probably can't afford to keep training new CIT officers when the old ones let their—clients? charges?—too close. You think you know her, but you feel empathy for her illness."

His vehemence raised doubts in her mind. He'd been a good soldier because he understood human behavior. He'd never screwed up a mission before because he'd been a good predictor. That much, she'd known about his job. It didn't change the fact that his reaction made her feel as if he had a stake in her life again. She couldn't let him think so.

"We're covering old ground. I don't want to talk about Janie."

"Fine, but if you let her back in, I'll take her out of here myself. You can ask Reverend Michael or someone she trusts to talk to her, but you're a cop who helps her when she needs a warm place to sleep. This is not her warm place."

"Liam must be good. He's helping you return to your old self in record time."

"Listen to me just this once. I know what I'm talking about, and you matter to me."

"No." She made herself look at them both with objective eyes. "You and I want all the power. My yes tops your no." She broke away from him. "We're friction, and we just keep hurting each other."

"Abby, wait." He took the steps in one jump, and stopped, so close his breath warmed her face. His eyes caressed, but he didn't touch her. A muscle jerked on the side of his throat. "I'm trying *not* to hurt you. Don't let whatever you feel for me stop you from being sensible about Janie."

"What I feel for you always makes trouble for me."

"I know." He let her shoulders go and stepped back, looking uneasy. "When I got here, you were singing at the top of your lungs with your windows wide open to the world. You let me in because you have faith I don't begin to understand. I don't want anyone to change you. When I leave, I want to know you still believe the best—even of me."

CHAPTER EIGHT

"ABBY? SOMETHING WRONG?"

She looked up from the paperwork she'd finished several minutes ago. Sergeant Macland waited, reports in his hand, impatient to be on his way home.

Abby scrambled to her feet. Her mind had been on her own life. "I'm fine."

"What happened other than those amateur prize fighters you brought in?"

"Nothing. It was quieter than usual except for the soccer dads." Abby watched him catalog the tear in her shirtsleeve and the grass stains on her knees.

The battling dads had disagreed about scoring in their sons' Friday-afternoon game. None of her male colleagues would have had to explain the brawl. She didn't, either. He could read her report if he got curious. She'd brought the men in, given them a lecture and a warning about assaulting each other and the police and sent them on their way.

"Good night, Sarge."

Pasting on a confident smile, she started toward the locker room. This used to be one of her favorite times of the day. Going home, maybe going out for drinks or dinner and shoptalk with her academy friends.

How she needed them now. Three weeks had passed since she and Thomas had shared their most serious conversation ever, and everything had subtly changed.

She opened her locker and took off her weapon.

Thomas seemed to stay with her all the time, in the back of her mind, either seducing her, or warning her about Janie. He'd made her more cautious.

Meeting the other woman at the door of Reverend Michael's shelter one afternoon, she'd waited for Janie to mention dropping by. Janie had said nothing about it, and Abby kept her silence, too. Now, she helped when Janie needed a hand, but she made no offer that brought the other woman back into her personal life.

It wasn't just work Thomas had disturbed. Her home felt less like her own. They maintained a polite distance, neither dangerous nor exciting. She ought to be grateful.

Thomas had started doing yard work each day. Abby wasn't sure if he wanted to earn his keep or make sure Janie stayed away. She never asked.

And he'd turned into a compulsive cleaner. His running clothes were always in her washing machine as he kept up a grueling exercise habit, but her house was immaculate.

Dinnertime had slowly changed from a lesson in enduring uncomfortable silence, into a nightly chat-fest. They talked about nothing and everything, and topped off each evening tidying the kitchen. She kept a bland smile ready and stopped asking how things went with Liam because Thomas seemed to think she was intruding.

All the while she reminded herself not to stare too long or listen too hard when he talked. He had his own life to return to. She had hers here. She'd tried to separate him from herself, and he obviously didn't want her mixing in with the sessions that were meant to send him back to North Carolina.

Liam must be doing him some good. He'd lost the bleak look that had lured her to his bed in the first place. If they could just get through a few more days—even weeks—Thomas would recover, go home and become a completely closed episode in her past. Living with her, helping out but never venturing over the line a housemate would toe, Thomas seemed to agree with the plan.

So she told herself as the days stacked up, one behind the other and her period didn't come. Never regular, she usually paid no attention. This month, with that night utmost in her mind, she'd had plenty of time to count back to the starting date of her last cycle.

She glanced around the locker room as she began to unbutton her shirt. The other women shared family news and work rumors. Abby had never let any of her other colleagues get as close as her academy friends—the group Lucy always called the six pack. What a relief it would be to share an uncomfortable truth with someone who cared.

She was probably carrying Thomas's baby.

Risa and Lucy would be shocked, but they'd try to understand. Christa and Mei would have to wonder out loud, much as she kept asking herself, how she'd been so foolish. Completely focused on their careers, they'd never have made a similar mistake.

Lucy and Risa and Crista had all begun new relationships, happy relationships headed toward marriage. They'd remind her she should be looking for the kind of joy they'd found, not settling for single motherhood, sharing a child with a man who'd already let her down.

She longed for the old days when she could phone them all with a time and a place and know they'd come, to cheer or jeer—but always to support.

Instead, she had to stop on her way home for a pregnancy test. If it came out negative, all the better. If she was pregnant, at least she'd know for sure. She'd better get used to being alone.

She finished changing into civvies and had just folded her uniform when her cell phone rang. As she answered, her mother was already talking, her voice high-pitched and rapid.

"Your dad and I want to talk to you. Meet us for dinner."

"Mom." Abby recognized the tone. Her mother was on the edge again. Abby steadied herself with a deep breath, but nearly choked on the musty scent of stale clothing and leather shoes. "How's class going?" Elaine always cut her schedule when her condition declined. The university's administration had understood her predicament and hired someone else to take over her classes when she was ill.

"I'm only teaching one course. Composition. You know I hate teaching composition." She spoke so fast she seemed to catch at gasps of oxygen between words. "I don't want to talk about school. Dad and I want to take you to dinner."

Her father's voice rumbled in the background. She wished he'd take the phone. At the same time, she prayed she hadn't triggered a new crisis for her mother by letting Thomas back into her life. Getting over him last time had taken so long both Abby and her mom had begun to think she might also suffer from an unnatural depression.

"Where do you want to meet?" Abby asked and wished she could add, "Are you taking your meds?"

"At Ripley's. It's only a few blocks from your house, but we'll still be private."

Meaning her parents could quiz her about Thomas without insulting him to his face. Abby glanced down at her flat stomach. Stress might be causing her problem. Maybe a night free of the intense awareness she felt around Thomas would bring on rescue from disaster.

On the way to the restaurant, she stopped at a pharmacy and bought a pregnancy test that she tossed into her back seat.

Waiting through two traffic-stalled red lights and three jaw-wrenching yawns, she considered calling her parents and canceling dinner. Once she sat still, with time to hope against fading hope that she wasn't carrying Thomas's child, she just wanted to go home and sleep.

Her parents had arrived at Ripley's before her. She parked behind their empty car and got out. Walking around her father's shiny black sedan, his pride and joy, she found an unscientific clue to her mother's condition. Her dad worked out his worry for her mom in the wax job. She could have put on makeup by the reflection in the metal surface.

She steeled herself and her muscles screamed, sore from her encounter with the soccer dads. While their wives had nearly also come to blows and their children had whimpered on the field beside them, she'd gone down in a tussle of arms and legs.

Facing her parents struck more fear in her than the men who'd dented her ribs and ripped the elbow out of her uniform shirt. She'd never been able to tell her mom and dad about her problems. They'd needed her to be calm and safe. That would never change as long as her mother's illness continued to rule the family.

Abby paused at the restaurant's door and reminded herself to smile. Taking a quick breath she went inside. Her parents surged at her out of the dim entrance.

"Sweetie." Her mom only called Abby pet names when she was also girding for battle. Her hug was more of a clench.

Abby hugged back, trying to share some of the serenity she was supposed to maintain. Then she disentangled herself and approached her father, using her eyes to plead for status on her mom. He shook his head, almost imperceptibly. What that meant, Abby couldn't say.

"Is there a line? Are we waiting?" She peered into the restaurant's dusky interior, but the hostess came around a wooden podium to greet them.

"All ready now?" she asked.

"We didn't want to sit without you," Elaine said to Abby.

Nodding, she brought up the rear of their small line wending through the faux-Tudor building where wood smoke and the aroma of cooked beef made her stomach jump.

She'd be glad to do that test after all. The only time she'd ever felt so consistently queasy had been during a two-day deep-sea fishing trip her father had insisted she'd love. Fortunately he'd held no grudge when she'd turned out to be a landlubber.

"Let's have wine." After they sat, her dad plucked the list out of a brass holder in the middle of the table. "I'll choose."

"None for me." Abby glanced at her mom, worried the truth was all over her face. "I took something for the pain in my elbow." She pulled back her sleeve.

It must look worse than she realized. Her mother slammed against the back of her chair. "That bruise covers your elbow and half your forearm."

"Two dads at a soccer game. They're a menace. And someone planted a fist in my ribs. Plus, they ruined my uniform. I'll have to replace both the shirt and pants."

"Abby." Just saying her name, her dad seemed to be suggesting she resign.

"It's fine." She pulled her sleeve back down. "Part of the job."

The waitress came and Abby ordered water with lemon. Her parents asked for the same.

"What we want to talk to you about—" her mom took advantage of their server's momentary absence "—is how long Thomas is staying. I called today, expecting he'd be gone by now, but he answered the phone. I asked him when he was leaving. He told me he still had time off."

Abby opened her mouth to suggest her mom shouldn't call Thomas to be rude, but then she slid a hand over her stomach. In her mother's place, she might be as aggressive. "He's taken no leave for a couple of years." He'd been working in dangerous places. "And he made a lot of friends when he was stationed at Ft. Hood."

"That's pretty far away. Wouldn't staying there have been a better idea?" Her father signaled to the server that they'd need a few more minutes.

"A lot of his friends are out of the Army now, and they live around here." The lie came, smooth as water.

"You understand why we want him gone?" Her father sounded more reasonable, but he was still less than polite.

Abby had spent her life trying to be the best daughter, to help where she could, but tonight placating her parents took too much energy. "What do you want me to say? Nothing's changed. Thomas is visiting. I have a house and he's welcome to stay. End of story." That pregnancy test floated into her mind, but she shoved it out of sight. "Try not to worry."

"Wait until you have children," her dad said. "You'll choke on that advice."

He hit too close to home and she softened. "If I start feeling funny about him, I'll come stay with you."

Her mother sat forward. "That's a great idea. Come home with us tonight. If Thomas is too cheap to rent a hotel room, he can luxuriate in your empty house and feel guilty for driving you out."

"Mom?" Abby tried not to laugh. Depending on her mother's mood, laughter could be an insult. "I'm fine in my house." Never better since Thomas had turned into a cleaning whirlwind. She might even leave a can of the living-room paint in his way. Her walls could use a touch-up.

Elaine shook her head. "You look tired." Falling ill again or not, she still possessed a mother's sharp eyes. "Maybe you're telling us the truth and your soccer dads wore you out, but you should take better care of yourself."

"Did you go to the E.R.?" her dad asked. "What if they broke your ribs?"

"One of the other dads at the field was a doctor. He looked us all over before I brought my guys back to the station. He seemed to assume I was a delicate flower."

"Even in your uniform?" Doubt lifted her mother's voice. "I wouldn't push you too far."

"Thanks, Mom." Abby curled her hand around Elaine's. "That's the nicest thing you've said since I joined the force." Her parents assumed she was one call away from getting killed or fired, as if their "little girl" wasn't cut out to be a cop. She'd hoped her mom would accept her job. Beaming, Abby released her mother's hand and took a closer look at the menu. "I'm starving."

Her father reached across the table. "I thought we raised you with more self-confidence."

"I'm confident." She peered over the top of the cardboard. "But everyone needs reassurance."

"My problems have forced you to be too responsible." Elaine grasped her husband's wrist, seeking a share of his strength.

"We do what we can as parents," he said. "Abby understands that."

"Mom, I'm not complaining." She rattled her menu again. "We're getting too serious. Let's just enjoy a meal together and not worry about what happens next."

Her mother's long sigh startled her. She put the menu down to find her mom slumped forward in her chair, braced against her forearms as if she couldn't hold up her own weight. The candle flickered, shaking from her impact against the table.

"Mom? Did I say something wrong?"

"I spend so much time worrying I'm going to embarrass you or your dad. Just getting through dinner without caring what anyone thinks sounds like the best idea I've ever heard."

To hell with the other diners. Abby circled the table and eased onto her bruised knees to wrap her arms around her mother.

"I love you," she said. "I hope I'm as good a mom as you one day."

Elaine shook, burying her face against Abby's shoulder. As her mom cried, Abby looked to her dad for support. He shook his head, his own eyes red.

"Mom?"

Elaine leaned back and brushed the hair from Abby's eyes, her palms loving and indulgent, despite the fact that the daughter she comforted was twenty-nine years old. "You didn't have a childhood. I wasn't capable of taking care of you always."

Abby pressed Elaine's hand against her face. "You're not allowed to say that. I'm not patting myself on the back, but look at me. I try to help people. I think before I speak because I don't want to hurt feelings. I have a good career. I own my own home and I pay my bills. Did you do such a bad job with me?"

Laughing through tears, Elaine glanced across at her husband, who took the hand she held out to him. "I guess she turned out pretty well, John?"

"I'm proud of her." He gripped Abby's shoulder, his voice ragged. "As long as she doesn't get us thrown out of here with a public display of affection."

Teasing him with an exaggerated sigh, Abby returned to her seat. Her father reached for her hand, too. His fond smile warmed Abby, but made her mother start crying again.

"We needed this," John said.

Elaine rummaged in her purse for a tissue.

"I needed you two." Abby couldn't tell them about her worst fear, but the pregnancy test in her car didn't frighten her as much now. Whatever happened, her parents had raised her to deal with the situation.

Her mouth dried. "Situation" hardly described a baby about to be born because she'd made a mistake.

THOMAS HAD LEFT HIS DOOR OPEN so he heard Abby come in. Sprawled on his bed, his arms crossed behind his head, he struggled with his temper. He had no right to worry about Abby. Being unable to think about anything else because she hadn't shown up at the normal time was irrational. Nevertheless, he rose from the bed, barely clinging to control.

He knew all the reasons he should keep his mouth shut. They'd worked hard to maintain a hands-off friendship over the past few weeks. She wasn't used to living with someone. Calling home to say she'd be late probably hadn't occurred to her.

But if she'd been the one waiting at home for him, she would have worried. He walked to the top of the stairs. Liam had told him to face his problems head-on. Abby certainly never ducked hers.

"Hey," he said.

She looked up, her eyes tired, a wad of dirty-looking uniform clenched between her elbow and side. A bag dropped out of the clothes and hit the floor. She snatched it up. "Huh?" Her faint smile took the edge off his hostility.

"I don't have the right to ask where you've been,

but maybe we could agree to call each other if we're going to be late?"

She looked apologetic. "I'm sorry. I'd have called the police by now if you were this late and you hadn't phoned." Her smile returned as she climbed the stairs with a more fluid gait than he expected. She paused at his side, and he smelled sunshine and fresh grass. "But no one's out to get me," she said.

"Don't try to tease me. I know I'm out of line, but I worried."

"You're right. I should have called, but you're upset for nothing. I was trying to distract you."

He had distracted her many times. He'd ignored her concerns and carried her to their bed as if she were the spoils of all his adventures. "Maybe." Hardly a quick-witted response, and it only focused her eyes on him.

"I just stopped to meet my parents for dinner. Have you eaten?"

A family meeting. That couldn't be good. They'd probably whipped out the hoses and hot lights. "How's your mom? She called today, but then she hung up on me. I hadn't decided whether to mention it." He felt for Elaine Carlton. "I'm making her worse?"

"She's not completely good, but she's not worse." At her protective response, he wished he hadn't said anything. "Maybe she's on edge, but she'll be all right." Abby lowered her head to hide her face. "But thanks for being concerned. She wouldn't understand or I'd tell her. G'night."

"Why wouldn't she understand?" Something was wrong. Abby seemed too anxious to get away from him.

"Mom would assume you felt more than you should for me."

The perfect defense. He took a deep breath, happy to let her go rather than discuss *feelings*. He did enough of that with Liam. But then she lifted her hand to push the door open and the bruise on her elbow caught him like a blow to the gut. "What happened to you?"

"Huh?" Her favorite word tonight, apparently. She twisted her arm as if she hadn't noticed it. "Oh, that. A fight at a soccer field."

"Kids bruised you like that?" He rocked in his shoes, trying hard to stay on his side of the hall, not check her for broken bones.

"I keep explaining this, but a couple of dads disagreed about a point between their sons' teams, and I got caught in the scuffle." She grinned, and her smiles began to look put-on. "I'm fine."

"Are you kidding me?" She looked up, a warning on her face. He wasn't allowed to do more than express surprise and then let it go. Their kind of "friendship" didn't allow for more. He snapped his mouth shut, but then he had to add, "You didn't let those guys go?"

"I took them downtown and explained that assaulting a police officer in front of their children wasn't a good idea."

He was overreacting. Again. "I'm sorry. You're good at what you do, but I'd learn to hate your job if I stayed much longer."

"Yeah. Well, I'm still not that thrilled with yours." She jumped, and he felt her cat's broad head pushing at his ankle. He didn't bother to look down, fascinated by an odd look of betrayal in Abby's eyes. "Herb's abandoned me since you came," she said.

"Because he's always in my stuff." The cat wound between Thomas's splayed feet. "I don't want pets." He'd never been a cat person, but Herb insisted on prowling through all of Thomas's personal goods, and he was always so interested, he kind of persuaded a man he might not be all bad. The cat grunted as if he read human minds, and Thomas tried to swallow a smile. He didn't want to like Abby's feline, but he could hardly shut the door in Herb's face every time he insisted on visiting.

"He sleeps with you, doesn't he? I can't find him at night anymore."

To his dismay, Thomas's face grew warm. He'd bet he'd never blushed in his life before. "In the room. We've reached an understanding. He stays in the armchair—off the bed—and I don't throw him out."

She looked as confused as her mother had that first day, but she recovered fast and continued into her room. If she'd had some gum, she'd have popped it like an old-time movie moll, pretending she didn't care. "Herb, I miss ya, buddy."

Grunting again, the cat lumbered toward Abby with a twitch of his plumed tail. Dropping her show of indifference, she greeted him with indecipherable baby talk and closed her door, shutting light out of the hall at the same time.

Loneliness swept Thomas, and he was bewildered. He couldn't talk to Liam about Abby, of missing her more than ever, now that she slept, untouchable, down the hall. He couldn't explain why only the warmth of her body next to his had taught him to sleep again.

And this…falling for a cat. It must be a side effect of PTSD.

Either that, or Liam's incessant palaver about how he *felt* must be getting to him. He shut his own door and turned on the small television Abby had provided. Better to catch up on the news than waste time guessing that putting up with the cat was safer than wanting Abby again.

ABBY BACKED OUT of the bathroom. When the back of her thighs hit the bed, she sagged onto it. Behind her, Herb purred like a mower engine.

Abby eyed the open bathroom door. It had to be a mistake. She'd thought she was used to the idea, or getting used to it.

Her head spun and she pressed both hands to her cheeks. Look again. Maybe she'd read it wrong.

On her feet, she hurried to the sink and grabbed the plastic stick she'd thrown in. She compared it to the test's instruction sheet again. No. It hadn't changed. And she hadn't read it wrong.

A positive pregnancy test.

It shouldn't be such a shock. She'd suspected—maybe feared—the worst almost from the moment she'd realized she hadn't taken precautions. Could a woman feel that she was pregnant so quickly?

No, but she'd been that afraid. Even before, when she and Thomas had been engaged, she would have been reluctant to tell him about a baby. His job took him out of the country more than he was home. His life was always at forfeit.

Father material? Not a chance. She'd been a sick woman's child, and she'd lived with all the self-doubt and fear that came with a family like hers. She wanted nothing like that to touch her child. Who knew if Thomas would ever really recover from his failed mission?

She turned toward her locked bedroom door. This problem didn't belong to him. She'd needed him that night, wanted him with all her heart. She refused to regret that now that she carried his child.

He hadn't known she wasn't using birth control. She'd made the mistake.

And now the consequences belonged to her.

Blood pounded in her ears. Thomas was in no shape to be her baby's father. How had she been so blind in those few moments that would have forestalled all this?

She reached for the phone, already reciting her parents' phone number in her mind. Then she stopped. Her mother, frenzied at the beginning of the evening, had wished her a calm good-night after they'd eaten and talked about the bland, lovely non-events of their everyday lives. No matter what she'd said to Thomas, Abby realized she might push her mother over the edge if she admitted she was pregnant. She had to find the right way to tell her mom.

Especially when she didn't need help. She rubbed her hand across her stomach. This was her baby.

Sweat trickled between Abby's breasts. Had she already decided not to tell Thomas? Ever?

Could she be so cruel?

A sudden knock on the door startled her. "Abby?" Thomas spoke softly, obviously trying not to wake her if she'd fallen asleep.

She stood, feeling braver about facing him on her feet. "Yes?"

"Are you sick or something?"

"No."

"I thought I heard you fall a few minutes ago."

She'd probably dropped that hard on her bed after careening away from the sink. "I'm—" She stared from wall to wall in her room. The paint, the pictures, nothing made a dent until she spied her ruined uniform in a heap by the closet door. "—sorting laundry." She flattened her palm across her forehead, expecting her brain to explode. "And shoes."

"Shoes?"

"I have to polish them before tomorrow." There. That was more like it. Her synapses were sparking again. She sat on the bed, returning to the small pool of light from the bathroom door. Pregnant. Tests weren't infallible. First things first. She'd do another one—or ten—tomorrow. "Then I'm going to bed. I might read."

"What's wrong with you?"

Her mouth appeared to be running on autopilot for one thing. "I'm tired from that call today. I don't like fistfights. I get upset and the adrenaline wears me out." That was no lie.

"You sound funny. Open the door and we'll talk."

Either that or she could crawl out her window like the coward she felt, knowing his child was growing inside her.

"I'm fine, Thomas. Don't worry."

He didn't answer. The way he walked without making a sound, she hoped he'd gone away.

"Are you sure?" He hadn't.

She faked a noisy yawn. "Yeah. Thanks, but I'm tired, and I have to get a new uniform ready. No big deal."

Holding her breath, she waited for him to finally

take the hint. This moment imprinted itself on her brain.

Night outside her window like a black curtain, her hands flat against the rough weave of her wine-red comforter. Thomas, waiting on the other side of the door, wanting to help, reluctant to leave her.

She couldn't face him yet. If she wasn't careful, she might tell him the truth.

At last he tapped on the door in disgust and then walked away. "Good night." From the sound of his voice, he'd already taken several steps down the hall.

She breathed again, air leaving her lungs in a whoosh that made her head spin faster. Panting for more oxygen, she thought she might be sick. Twenty-nine years old, and she'd desired Thomas so much she hadn't remembered to keep herself safe.

And what about him? He didn't deserve a lifetime obligation. He'd come to her for help, not father-hood.

CHAPTER NINE

"DADDY, WHY DO WE HAVE TO pull these flowers out, but leave those in?"

The voices came from the other side of Abby's faded wooden fence. On her knees, pulling her own weeds since about sunrise, she wondered what had driven her neighbor out this early with his young daughter to tend their yard.

"This kind isn't flowers," the man said, "but that one you just pulled is. Those are the ones we want to leave in the ground."

"I can't tell, Daddy." A touch whiny, the little girl grunted and a sound, something plastic hitting glass, made her father "shush" her.

"Don't throw your trowel. Mommy and Kyle are sleeping."

"Whattsa trowel?"

Abby sat back on her heels, queasy as she remembered the lady next door had been heavily pregnant. She pictured that family—a mother and a father who would help with the hard work of raising children.

Behind Abby, on the picnic table, her portable

phone rang. She jumped, peeling off her gloves, and crawled to the table on her knees. She grabbed the phone before it could ring a second time. Thomas might already have left for his run, but he might still be asleep.

"Hello?"

"Abby, this is Trey Norse. My wife's gone into labor. Can you take my shift tonight?"

Suddenly, her world was one baby after another.

"Tonight?"

"I'm sorry it's short notice, but I've asked everyone else."

Meaning the guys who could better handle a shift on the street that boasted the most bars in Houston. Abby jumped on any task that kept her from thinking about what to do next. "Sure, Trey. Glad to do it. Are you calling from the hospital?"

"Yeah, and if I don't get back to the labor room, Libby'll kill me."

"Good luck." She'd be in Libby's place—alone—when her own child came. How good would she be with pain? "I hope the baby's healthy."

"Thanks, Abby. I'll let you know."

"Good." She hung up, hoping he'd remember. Most guys rarely shared anything about their personal lives with her. She and her friends had often discussed the men's impromptu pool games after work, their caffeine wind-downs at Bert's Coffee Pot on the way out of town from the station.

Abby didn't know one woman who'd been in-
cluded.

She pushed the phone onto the table. Baby news
was better than nothing—and it might prove to be a
way into the men's world her colleagues guarded
like little boys with a tree house.

"What's up?"

She turned. "Thomas, don't you ever make a
sound?"

Around them, the morning breeze rippled through
live oak leaves. Traffic whispered past on the sur-
rounding streets. In the next yard, the dad had persuaded his little girl to take the conversation to a
lower tone, but she was still plying him with questions about butterflies and clover and "Why does
Kyle sleep so much anyway?"

Thomas would have had to wear a bell around his
neck to warn her he was coming.

He stopped at her side. "Want to talk about whatever's bothering you? You're not the kind of woman
who snaps at a man for walking through the yard
without knocking down the house."

She couldn't talk to him with his damp T-shirt
clinging to his chest, and his shorts skimming thighs
whose texture her palms remembered. Rough hair
against smooth skin.

Power to take what he wanted with his bare body,
though he'd never used his strength against anyone
except an enemy. Half the reasons she wanted him

were also reasons to distance herself. His strength had kept him from needing anyone, and she'd been attracted, back when she hadn't known she wanted him to need her.

Now, he might need more than she'd be able to give. She didn't want her child to know a moment of fear. Even if Thomas was no longer the hollow man who'd come to her door, his life would require his child to grow up fast.

"Nothing's wrong." She stared straight into his eyes, daring him to call her a liar. She had a lot to hide now. "I have to take a guy's shift tonight so I'll be out."

"Okay," he said with that strange frown he wore so much lately. "Sure you feel like it?"

She felt numb. "I'm fine."

"What about those bruises? You must be sore."

She was tender all right, but not physically. She yanked a weed out by its roots. "Just fine."

After a few moments, she turned around. Thomas had gone. What a relief. She'd face him in a day or two, but right now, she felt at fault for getting pregnant and worse for not telling him.

A doorbell rang. Sounded as if it came from her house. She prayed her parents hadn't come to check on her.

Instead Liam came through the door Thomas held as if he were the host around here. Liam didn't seem to notice. From the porch, he looked her over. Thomas must have ratted her out.

"What's up with you?" Liam asked.

She glared at Thomas. "You're feeling subtle today."

"You set up my once-a-day visits because you're worried about Thomas. He's simply returning the favor." With a sheepish grin, Thomas returned to the kitchen. "Something's bothering you," Liam said. "I see trouble written all over you."

She made no effort to hide her growing sense of claustrophobia. "You people are crowding me." She didn't mean to sound testy, but... "What do I have to do for a little privacy?"

Liam laughed. "You can start by not looking as if someone dragged you backward through your own hedge."

"I had a fight with some guys at a soccer game yesterday. You know how I hate fights."

He made room for Thomas, who'd returned with a cup of coffee for him and another he brought down to Abby.

Coffee. Caffeine. Nursing it long enough to keep either man from noticing she'd just cut caffeine from her diet should be easy. "Thanks." She carried it toward the house, but offered them the picnic table with a beckoning hand. "I'll go get the paper while you two start your session."

"I brought it in before I left. Mr. Pfeiffer and I are getting to be friends, though he still balks when I suggest he should stop stealing it." Thomas cracked a grin. "I offered to use a little muscle, but he's feisty for an old guy. He's sure he could take me."

Liam's head snapped around so quickly Abby wondered what the hell Thomas had been telling him about his time in the desert. Thomas looked from Liam's wary face to Abby, and they both laughed.

"He's kidding, Liam." She and Thomas had once shared a talent for finding humor, even in the crises of the lives they couldn't blend. If only she dared congratulate Thomas on making a joke. He might not be well enough to take that much teasing. "You haven't canvased the rest of the neighborhood to scare off dangerous characters?"

"No." But he looked guilty.

Damn. "You've been looking for Janie."

"Someone has to." With a glance at Liam, he nodded toward the house. "Let's start."

THOMAS IMAGINED hauling Liam across the table and shutting his mouth once and for all. He'd grown tired of sweating under the man's nonstop questions.

"We're getting nowhere, Thomas, and I'm giving you more hints than I usually give patients."

"I'm that lucky, huh?" He slid his hand around the back of his neck. "Here's the thing. I've been over what happened so many times I recite it in my sleep. Why do you think that helps? I haven't forgotten, and the fact that I tried to protect you from Janie doesn't make me feel better."

"Yet you are feeling better?"

Thomas breathed in the baked-apple-and-fresh-coffee scent. As familiar as the story Liam insisted he narrate over and over. "Yeah, I'm better, but I don't know that you have anything to do with the improvement."

Liam nodded. "You're thinking it's because Abby's let you stay in her perfect little home here."

"You're being sarcastic about her?"

"Something can look and smell perfect and still be flawed. Maybe the way to your heart is all those apple candles she likes so much, but it's not the way to fix the fight going on in your head."

"It's not the damn candles. She accepts me, and she doesn't mind that I'm not the same as I was."

"She likes that you're not the same." Liam looked resentful. "She loves to heal the sick and provide shelter for lost souls."

"My soul's lost." Though he'd glimpsed a piece of it in Abby's smile in the garden.

"So you're perfect for her."

"Now who's overreacting? She's not going to take me back. I wouldn't even ask her. Everything's different now. She's not young enough to believe I'll change." He swallowed, made a better man by the truth he'd avoided since that night they'd spent together. "And I'm not selfish enough to risk hurting her again."

Liam widened his eyes. Thomas almost laughed.

Now would be the time to strike if Liam were the bomb-strapped woman in the living nightmare he faced every day. She'd never been shocked to see him, or afraid of what he'd do. He'd been the one who couldn't understand what was happening as she'd begged him to save her children. Before Thomas could think straight again, a man in her own family had set off the bomb by remote control.

Liam exhaled, giving up. "Here's my gift to you. The truth about that story you keep telling me. First, it's not a story. It's part of your life, and you are going to have to live with it. Second, you had no choice. You came upon a woman whose family was about to kill her for the joy of taking you and your squad out, too."

A pain behind Thomas's right eye made him blink. Familiarity with the details had made him accept it without quite the level of panic he'd felt before Liam. "There had to be another choice. I'm trained to make better choices."

"Thomas, you would have found it by now if it existed. You hate needless violence as much as Abby. You want to lead dispassionately, but you can't separate yourself from being afraid and angry that your friends and that woman—"

"And her children," Thomas said through gritted teeth.

"When they died, the part of you that could shut down your emotions to do the job took a hit. You can mend it, but not until you forgive yourself. You had no choice, and you'll have the same options if you go back."

"I'm going back." His palms began to sweat as he saw himself on one of the transports. He knew the drill too well, and he wasn't ready.

"So you tell me."

"Give me other options."

"I won't be with you when someone else with a bomb tries to kill you or his own innocent family."

"Nothing changes?"

"Not until you realize you deserve to live." Liam propped his feet on the coffee table. "You won't even let yourself care about Abby because you're not sure you'll come back."

Thomas scrambled to his feet and paced to the window. "You're the wrong man to talk to me about Abby."

"Something's different between you. When you first arrived, you two kept your distance. In the garden, you took the same side to laugh at me on the other."

Thomas felt sick.

Liam shook his head without looking directly at Thomas. "I'm not jealous."

"Sure you are." Liam's envy would ease Thomas's conscience for sleeping with Abby after their first session. "You don't want to imagine how Abby was with me, and I feel the same about you. I'm grateful you're willing to go through this with me, but I'd have talked to Mr. Pfeiffer before you if I'd thought he could help."

"Okay, I'm done." Liam lifted his feet, careful not to scrape the table as he put them down.

The smirk was finally gone, but Thomas had the feeling he should have been nicer—or something. "Liam, I didn't come here to be with her."

"I disagree." Liam dropped all pretense of friendship. "You don't know what you want, but you didn't have to come to Houston. I'm not the only doctor who wouldn't break confidentiality. You came because Abby's here. When you no longer wanted to live, but you hated wanting to die, you came to Abby."

"No."

"That's why you refuse to see you can be okay. She matters so much to you that you won't risk losing her. You can't go back to work, and you can't make a future for yourself."

Rage, slow yet powerful, stole over Thomas like a large, smothering hand. "That's bullshit." He couldn't say more with his heart pounding toward his head, blinding him, cutting off his breath.

"It is," Liam agreed. "Because I would have given Abby more, but she didn't want me." Before Thomas could get his hands on Liam, the other man turned on his heel. "I'll be back on Monday. I can't talk to you until then."

Thomas didn't trust himself to move. That day

after the bomb had gone off, he'd aimed his weapon at the sky and fired. He would have killed anything that moved, and he felt the same now.

He had pride. "Don't bother to come back" would have felt damn good, but Liam had helped him. If he refused to talk again, he might never find a way back to his old life. He'd made a commitment, and his men deserved better from him.

THE NIGHT WAS CALM until another patrol unit asked for backup at the Tip One Up bar on Cordero. Abby called in, gave her ETA and then headed over with siren and lights.

She put her own problems out of her mind. Bar fights, usually based on big talk, often turned into mayhem.

She squealed to a stop in front of the bar, along with two other cars. One was a single, like her. The other carried a rookie she'd seen around the station, and a more experienced patrol officer. The noise hit them before they hit the doors. Shouting—women's screams—shattering glass. The beer company sign beside the entrance suddenly shattered over them.

Abby pushed through the double swing doors, her nightstick already in one hand. Drowning in shouts and music too loud to yell over, she and her fellow officers fanned out and began dividing the reeling bodies, like bits of yarn tied in come-to-life knots.

Abby stumbled over a fallen stool, gagging as

the stench of stale beer hit her almost palpably in the face. More glass shattered on the wall behind her head. A shard sliced her neck on a ricochet. One man's voice rose above all other sounds.

"Damn you all. You'll listen or I'll kill ya. He died, and someone killed him. I saw someone kill him."

"He ain't dead." The bartender waved a bat in the shorter, stocky belligerent's face. "You just cold-cocked him with your Shiner Bock."

"Yeah, and it's a sad waste of good beer. Pass it thisaway if you're not drinking." Some helpful good old boy made the offer, but it helped. The men in the room paused to laugh.

"You lump of sh—" The guy the bartender had menaced with his bat went after the good old boy.

"Hey, hey." One of the cops caught him by the collar. "There are ladies present. Why don't we take this outside?"

Instead, the smaller man forced an elbow toward the patrolman's face, and all hell broke loose again.

"Wait!" Abby waded in, heading for the drunken instigator. She might be able to help him if he didn't get himself killed first. A blow to the stomach sent her back a step, but she surged forward again. "Don't use your club on him," she shouted to the patrolman who'd found his nightstick and was aiming it to-ward the loudmouth's head. Rather than rendering him unconscious, they might want to find out if he'd really seen someone commit murder.

She ducked another chair and came upright again at the patrolman's side in time to wrench his nightstick arm down. "Stop." She had to yell. "Didn't you hear what he said?"

"Before he tried to feed me his elbow? Yeah."

She grabbed the drunk's other arm. As he writhed between them, still muttering about killers, she heard the word *poison*.

"Unless y'all all want to spend the night in a cell, everybody shut up. Now." The patrolman was taller than most everyone else in the room, and his voice boomed loud enough to intimidate.

The other combatants took him at his word, and the noise level began to subside as Abby's colleagues managed to separate the roiling knots of men and women.

Abby hung on to the drunk guy, who was still muttering about poison and no one listening.

"What's he talking about?" She held on to the other cop's nightstick, which he also gripped in one hand as he struggled with their catch. He dropped the stick only to apply his handcuffs. "Were you here first?" she asked, patting the drunk down for weapons.

The patrolman didn't answer initially. The floor of the bar was a restless surge of humanity, slowly calming down, but not yet stable. Nearby, at least two men, in jeans and Western plaid flannel shirts, had stopped to listen.

"Yeah, I got here first," the patrolman said. "Who are you?"

"Officer Carlton, *CIT*," she said.

His narrowing gaze noted her emphasis. "He's not one of your—" He seemed to have an insulting name in mind, but he didn't use it. "He's not sick. He's drunk." With a sour face, he shook his head. "I've never smelled a guy so drunk."

Abby let go of the nightstick to catch a man falling toward them. "He's upset. I say we listen to his story."

"Hey, cut it out." The rookie, losing his temper, bellowed, and at last it worked. All movement finally stilled. The young guy looked startled as the patrons and the other cops turned his way. Nervous laughter greeted his surprise.

"That's more like it," the first patrolman said. "Now let's sort out who gets to spend a night in city accommodations." He got in front of the trouble-maker. "You. Will you talk to this officer? She's helped guys like you before and she cares if you get hurt tonight." He bent his head toward Abby, but looked their guy in the eye. "Otherwise, I'm throwing you in the back of my car, and I don't care what brought you here."

The man tried to put out his cuffed hand, trembling with adrenaline or maybe hunger. "I'm Harv Stuckey."

The patrolman shook hands and turned toward Abby. "His name mean anything to you?"

"Not yet."

"Put him in your car."

Abby lifted an eyebrow. The rules said that the first cop to the scene was the lead, but this guy took his assumed responsibility too seriously. "Thanks for all the advice."

"Look, I just don't want him to hurt you."

"I'm fine." She was half tempted to drag Harv through the bar, but the other cop's chauvinism wasn't his fault. "What say we go, Harv?" She looked back, the spirit of revenge pushing her. "Sure you can handle this situation?"

Her colleague laughed. "I'll have plenty of backup."

She assisted Harv through the melee he'd created. "What about this murder, Harv?"

"You don't believe me. No one believes me. I called the cops."

"If you tell me, I'll listen. Maybe we'll check it out together."

"I'm not that drunk, lady."

She shoved him past the last interested spectator, glass crunching beneath their feet. "Officer. You can call me Officer."

"Doesn't matter what I call you. You're gonna ignore me like everyone else. A guy doesn't have a home to go to—people act like he's a half-wit—like he's not even human."

"I wouldn't do that." They reached her car and she opened her back door. "Here you go. I have to leave the cuffs on you." Who knew if he'd lose control again?

"It's okay. I've worn them before."

She helped him inside, sheltering his head from the metal doorframe. He immediately shifted to make his wrists more comfortable and put his head back. He had spent time cuffed in the back seat of a cop's car before.

He seemed to fall asleep. He looked unconscious by the time she called in his name to check for warrants.

He'd visited the drunk tank six times in the past year. Which meant he'd been drunk a lot more often than even his record indicated.

She glanced back at him in the rearview mirror. Tomorrow, when he was sober, she'd drop by the station and ask him about treatment for his drinking.

"I'm not asleep. I'm serious. I'll tell you, but you're my last try. I've spent a year trying to make someone believe me."

"So you said."

"I'm not trying again after tonight. Not even if I see that guy die in my head every day for the rest of my life."

He talked like Thomas, which tended to convince her he was telling the truth. "Harv?"

"Whaddaya want?"

"Your story." He was angry, desperate, full to the eyes of secrets he'd been forced to keep. "I can't do anything about it if you don't tell me."

"I was walking in Memorial Park."

"We're talking about a murder?"

Her faith in his honesty took an immediate dip. A murder in the park and the cops wouldn't believe him? He couldn't have been the only witness.

"Who died?" Abby asked.

"That—" he stopped to press his finger over his mouth "—I can't tell you."

"You told everyone in the bar before we got there."

"But I'm not as drunk now. I don't want to die, too."

"Someone's after you?" she tried to believe because he was so serious.

"No shit."

"Who's after you, Harv? Who died?"

"Maybe you'll be able to figure it out. Shut up and let me say what happened."

"A little respect, Harv."

"I didn't tell anyone what I saw at first. I couldn't believe it, and I was scared—like a little kid. Too scared to talk. Who listens to a man like me? I might as well be a ghost."

She shuddered. Janie all but took pride in her refusal to live in society, but Harv felt his isolation. And she knew his chances on the street. Even in a climate as friendly as Houston's, he was subject to ill health and crime. "This other guy?" She cleared her throat. She'd learned never to ask a man what brought him to the streets. No one wanted to share that story until trust came into the picture—and she'd only let herself know Janie that long or closely.

"I called 911, but the operator wanted my name. What would it matter? She wanted my address." His laughter ended on a sound much more like a sob. "I called a bunch of times that first night, but they wanted my name. So I tried to forget." He slumped, his head falling forward. Immediately, he grunted and inched to the side as if he'd hurt his arms. "You can't hide from the truth. That guy's face was all over the paper. Every paper in town and that national one. I saw one morning as I bought a—one of those—you know—a bagel."

She ignored his slurring. "You knew this man's name?"

"Not till I saw the paper. He ran by me, drinking from one of those sports drinks. In a plastic bottle? I noticed 'cause I was thirsty. Then he passed out of sight behind some trees." Harv's voice deepened. He was watching this old movie in his head. "When I went around the trees I caught up with him. Get that? He was running. I was walking. I caught up— because by then he was staggering. I asked him if he needed help. You know, guys that age, out running? He looked at me like I was going to mug him."

"Are you saying—" Abby couldn't finish. Her own heart had started a sluggish drumbeat in her throat. She knew a man who'd died in Memorial Park, running.

"I'm saying they killed him. The papers said heart attack. He'd dropped that bottle so I picked it up—it was almost empty. But that day was damn hot. He needed fluids."

"Fluids?" It didn't sound like a Harv-word. She had to know if someone had coached him, especially if he meant... Jordan's face had been all over the papers. Even the national ones.

"I used to be an EMT. Whaddaya think? He drank some more. We were standing there, just standing. He looked at me funny. I don't know if he couldn't talk or he wouldn't, but all of a sudden, he dropped. He froze up, like someone had stuck battery cables in his fists. Then he had some sort of—" he struggled with the word "—convulsion." It came out in several carefully enunciated syllables. "And then he died."

A cold chill made Abby shiver. "Convulsions?" She knew this story too well. She'd heard it because of who it was. Jordan, Catherine Tanner's husband.

"You don't have convulsions when you have a heart attack. I couldn't find a—heartbeat. I ain't got one of those cell phones, so I ran to find a public phone and call 911. When I came back, the bottle was gone."

"Gone?"

"I don't know why I noticed, but I did."

"And that made you think he was poisoned?"

"I knew he was once they said he had a heart attack in the papers. You don't have convulsions when you have a heart attack."

"Why didn't you say anything?"

"To the paramedics? I did."

"Afterward, when you saw the papers."

"They killed him. You think they couldn't kill me?"

"Killed him? I can't believe— You didn't take the bottle?"

"I'd give anything to make the cops test that bottle."

"*Make* them? You're saying the police botched the investigation?"

"Did you know they murdered him?"

"I still don't. Forgive me if I'm wrong, but how do I know you're not after attention?" She glanced at him, but she didn't have the heart to meet his eyes for long. "If you'd sold that story to a tabloid, you'd be off the street."

"Come on. I told you." He bounced against the seat in frustration. "I called the cops. All the time. They didn't want to hear it."

"Then why did you keep trying?"

He laughed, a sound so harsh it nearly took off the roof of her car. "Look at me. I'm invisible. I have to throw chairs around a bar before I can make people listen. That guy never got justice. He was invisible, too, 'cause no one knows. If I don't make someone hear, he dies with no one to take his side."

"And you called 911 again after that day?"

"For a few weeks. Then I went to the station. They said I was talking gibberish and threw me out. One night, I'm in a bar, and this guy comes in. A cop. In uniform."

"Who was it?"

"The cop in the bar, or the dead guy? I can't say either name in this car. Nobody kills a guy like that alone."

"A guy like who? Say the name."

"You don't know? What kind of cop are you?" He kicked at the seat. Abby didn't blame him. "I should have gone with Pistol Pete back at the bar."

"Pistol Pete wouldn't believe you because the guy you're talking about did have a heart attack. The M.E. said so." She felt sick as her stomach roiled. His desperate efforts had put him in danger if he was right. But he couldn't be right. "What did the cop in the bar say? How did he identify himself?"

"As the sonofabitch who'd kill me if I didn't shut my mouth."

She hit the brakes, but then let off. "Were you drunk already when he came in?"

"His name's Fontanero. A sergeant. He didn't tell me. I read it on his uniform. He said if I wanted to live, I'd better stop talking about the guy with the heart attack."

Eddie Fontanero. Dirty all the way to his eyebrows. How he got away with it, no one knew, but he was rumored to be one of Buster Rialto's men. And Buster Rialto got every building contract the city offered.

"Are you sure about him, Harv?"

"Are you drunk, too? Hell, yes, I'm sure. And if the medical examiner wasn't in on the deal, he did the autopsy wrong."

"Couldn't the convulsions have caused a heart attack?" She had to ask him about Fontanero when he was sober.

"Poison caused the convulsions and the man died."

"How much did you drink tonight?"

"I drink this much for fun." Harv's lighter laughter, edging on hysteria, mocked her.

"Who have you told before? Give me names."

"You give me one, and we'll talk."

He meant the victim. She took a deep breath. Even thinking his name hurt because Catherine, once her mentor at the academy, the wise woman of their small, broken group of friends, had already suffered enough over her husband's death. She groaned. Pain blossomed from the pit of her stomach again. "Jordan," she said. "Jordan Tanner."

"Bingo."

Abby stared at him in her mirror.

"I'm drunk because I saw a guy die, and I stopped trying to do anything about it after Fontanero. Since then I drink a lot. I need the liquid courage to make someone see that man yelling from his grave, 'cause if you get killed, someone should find out why."

With a wrench of the steering wheel, Abby pulled to the side of the road. The seat belt. Suddenly, the release refused to work. She barely plunged free of the car before she doubled over to be sick on the road's shoulder.

And then she remembered. The baby. And the blow to her stomach.

On an agonized wave of fear, she was sick again.

CHAPTER TEN

SHE HAD TO GET TO A HOSPITAL without letting anyone in the department know she was going. She couldn't remember how she'd found out Risa was there after her partner's shooting, but the information had spread through the air with a life of its own. A cop shot, and his partner in the E.R.

That night she'd obeyed a compulsion to join her friends as they'd waited to make sure Risa was all right. She'd give almost anything to have them with her now, the way they used to be, easing her mind with the unconditional support that had once been their collective talent. Unfortunately, that shooting had made their support conditional indeed, and they couldn't seem to find a way back to their friendship from the barriers that had risen when they'd all gone their own ways.

Each of them had secrets to keep, a career to protect, a flaw she hadn't recognized before. Abby couldn't let anyone else find out about her pregnancy now. She didn't want Thomas to know, and she didn't want anyone else to interfere, even with well-meaning advice.

Abby straightened and looked back at her car.

Muffled sobbing came faintly through the open door. Abby wiped her mouth and wished she could cry, too. She marched back and slid behind the steering wheel, holding her stomach.

"What's wrong, Harv?"

"You're the first person to believe me, and obviously, you're scared, too. Fontanero's no one to play with."

"I'm not scared. If you can still tell me your story in the morning when you're sober, we'll find a way around Fontanero."

"If you're not scared, why are you puking all over the road?"

A punch to her gut might have killed her baby. As much as she cared for Catherine, her baby came first. "My stomach's upset."

"One thing I've found out since that guy dropped at my feet—you cops are all too dumb to pay attention. Now that I've told you, you're in danger, too. If someone finds out, how safe will you be?"

"You could have read about Fontanero in the papers. He makes them often enough."

"I thought you believed me. This Tanner guy haunts me. Tell me now if you're not going to do anything, either."

Another cramp gripped her. She took a deep breath and endured. "Did you ever talk to anyone in Homicide?" Had he called Catherine? She couldn't ask. If he was unbalanced, she shouldn't give him the idea that he should get in touch with her friend.

"I've called Tanner's paper. I've called the guy's wife. I couldn't talk to her, though."

"You called and hung up?" On Catherine's behalf, she was angry. "That probably made her feel good."

"I wanted to tell her, but how do you say a woman's husband's been murdered?" He rolled his head on the back of the seat. "Especially if you didn't do anything to help him? If you let the killer get away with it all." The last word trailed out of his mouth.

Despite the pain in her stomach, Abby concentrated on driving the last few miles to the station. After she parked, she turned around. "Harv, I promise I'll follow up. When we go inside, I'm going to ask a friend to book you for being drunk and disorderly. You'll be safe in one of our cells for the night."

"Unless Fontanero hears I'm here, and I talked to you. Don't you do anything that gets me killed."

She almost vomited again. He'd lived with this nightmare for a year. If he was telling the truth, his story meant a whole new nightmare for Catherine. And if the killer was a cop, it meant Jordan Tanner had planned to report something harmful to the department.

"Just don't talk. Keep your head down and get some sleep."

Dizziness swept her, but she struggled out of the car and opened the back door for Harv. He stood, but then pulled her to a stop. She looked at him, her mind on her own body. She didn't think she was bleeding.

"Let's move, Harv."

"I wanna…" His jaw worked. He looked away from her and then back. Alcohol fumes rolled past Abby's face. "Thanks."

"For putting you in jail?"

"You believe me?"

"I don't know." She tried never to lie. "But I understand what you mean about being haunted." If Thomas hadn't come to her, would she have ignored Harv, too?

"Why aren't you booking me yourself?"

"I'm sick." She prayed she made it to the hospital before she had to stop again. She prayed her baby was all right. "I'll come back in the morning. If they release you first, go to the cafeteria, and I'll meet you."

"No." He looked up at the building with doubt. "I won't hang around in there. Two streets over. That café the bookie runs. I'll meet you there."

Bookie? Breakfast should be eventful. "If I don't show up by ten o'clock, call this number." If something was wrong with the baby she might not be able to meet Harv. She pulled her card from her pocket and flipped it over to write her cell phone number on it. "We'll set up another meeting."

"Okay." He put the card in his own pants pocket. "But I'll see you tomorrow."

In the station, Abby scouted for a trusted face. Doug Saunders, a patrolman who'd been in her academy class the second time around, looked as if he was returning to his car.

"Doug?"

He stopped, his cap in hand. "Hey, Abby, it's been a long time."

"I'm taking Trey Norse's shift tonight, but suddenly I'm not feeling too well. Could I ask you to book my friend Harv, here?"

Harv looked startled that they were suddenly such buddies, but Doug nodded. "Sure, what've you been doing tonight, pal?"

"Drunk and disorderly," Harv said with dignity that tugged at Abby. The guy had real problems, but if his story was true, the past year had only made them worse.

"Be nice, Doug." She took off Harv's cuffs. "Okay? And don't noise his name around?"

"Sure." Doug looked interested, but he was a good cop. He asked no unnecessary questions.

Quiet now and amenable to a night in a clean bed, however noisy it might be, Harv went with the other man.

Abby explained she was sick to the watch commander and left as fast as she could walk without causing any further comment. She drove like a bat out of hell to the hospital her family always used.

Parking illegally at the emergency-room entrance, she ran inside. A nurse looked up from the admission desk.

"Abby, what's wrong?"

She'd brought so many people here the staff knew her. It didn't matter. "Tina, I'm pregnant, and I was in a bar fight about an hour ago and someone hit me in the stomach. I'm having cramps, and I threw up a couple of times." Tears clouded her eyes. She tried not to let them go, but she couldn't hold back. Her baby… "I don't want to lose my baby."

Tina raced around the desk. "Come with me."

"Aren't you supposed to stay at your desk?" Abby looked back, but Tina was already hauling her by the arm.

"I know where the ultrasound machine is." Tina turned down a wide hall and pulled Abby past several treatment areas. "How far along are you?" Without waiting for an answer, she pushed her arm through the bent elbow of a scrubs-suited man leaning on a counter. "Pete, this is Abby if you don't know her. She's pregnant. She's suffered a blow to the abdomen, and she's having cramps."

"I know Abby. How many weeks are you?" Pete asked.

"About four."

"The ultrasound might at least show us the sac. We won't be able to tell much, but we'll run it now, and then we'll run it again in a week or so. Are you bleeding?"

"I don't think so."

"Let's make sure about that. I'll take a urine sample and run a pregnancy test. Tina, better find a doctor. We'll treat her for shock anyway."

Their concern made hers more real. She couldn't seem to stop crying as she gave them the sample and the technician settled her on the bed to run the ultrasound. The woman patted her arm gently with her free hand as she ran the ultrasound probe around Abby's belly.

"Don't worry. You did everything right by coming here."

"What do you mean?" The woman seemed to be comforting her already. Hot tears poured down Abby's cheeks. "No" screamed through her mind. She couldn't lose this baby before she'd even been happy to have it. Her heart ached. Pain as heavy as granite pinned her to the hard bed. "Is it over?"

"What? I've hardly started."

"My pregnancy." Abby knew beyond any doubt that she wanted her child. This baby was part of her and Thomas—her family and his. She couldn't lose it. "Am I—"

"Aah, there we are." The woman, about Abby's mom's age, pointed at the screen. "See that? It's the amniotic sac, and that's your baby. We can't see movement or a heartbeat yet, but you're definitely pregnant."

Relief flooded her. "Would you know if I'm losing it now?"

The woman avoided looking at her. "No, but we'll run the test again in a week."

"That's what Pete said. What are you looking for?"

"By next week we'll see growth when we compare the two scans." The woman patted her again. "Try not to worry. You won't do yourself any good, and you need to stay healthy for your baby."

A new flood of tears cut off her ability to talk.

"Can I call someone for you?" the woman asked.

Pete and Tina and this new woman—all comparative strangers who wanted her to be okay, but they didn't love her. They didn't know her. "May I use the phone?"

"Sure." The woman stood, discreetly not asking where the baby's father might be. "I'll find the doctor."

Abby dialed her own parents' house. Luck held and her father answered. "Dad." Courage failed her. She could wade into a bar fight any day, but her father would not be thrilled that she'd been this careless.

"Abby, what's wrong?"

He already knew she was in trouble. How lucky was she to have someone who loved her that much? She was usually so busy trying to protect her parents from any extra stress, she tended to forget the three of them constituted a whole family. "I need you. Try not to worry, but I'm at St. Anselm's, in the emergency room. Can you come?"

"Are you hurt?"

"I'm not sure, but be careful with Mom."

"Is this part of the job, Abby?"

Nausea rolled over her with the force of a tank. She spoke past more tears than she'd cried in her entire life. "No, Dad, it's not part of the job. I'm scared, and I need you."

"Tell me no one shot you."

"No—I'm sorry—I didn't mean to make you think that, but I don't want to tell you what's wrong over the phone."

"Your mother is beside me. I think you have to tell us."

"I'm pregnant, and someone hit me in a bar fight. Please hurry up, Dad."

"On my way."

Thank God. Whatever happened, they'd be together. She shied away from thoughts of Thomas. He had rights she couldn't face now. First, she had to make sure her baby was all right and she didn't drive her mother into another downswing. "Be gentle with Mom."

"You take care of yourself. Lie back and don't think about anyone else. We'll be right there."

She hung up the phone as someone knocked on the door. Before she could say *come in,* the door opened and another woman walked inside.

"I'm Dr. Clegner." She shook hands. "Your test is positive," she said, "and the ultrasound shows us you're four weeks pregnant."

"Is my baby okay?"

"I don't see why not. You aren't bleeding. We don't think you're in shock, though I'd like to see you with your feet up tonight. You were fighting in a bar?"

She'd traded her uniform for a hospital gown. "I'm a police officer. I stopped a fight in a bar."

"You're a cop?"

Abby nodded. "When will you know if I'm all right?"

"If I weren't concerned about shock, I'd let you go home." She picked up Abby's chart and made a few notes. "Have you called the father?"

"No." But now that she'd let him into her head, she couldn't force him out again. He had every right to know his child might be in danger. Except that he'd never considered he was making a child.

The other woman nodded, her eyes pensive. "Okay. Is anyone bringing you pajamas?"

"And comfort? My parents are on their way, but I didn't think to ask for pajamas."

"About your job—" Instead of continuing, the doctor stopped with a self-conscious smile.

"My job?" Didn't she take enough chauvinism from the men at work?

"I was going to say I wouldn't want to be a cop while I was pregnant, but a kid on PCP kicked me in the stomach in the E.R. when I was twelve weeks along with my youngest daughter. Have the good sense to ask for a desk assignment if you ever feel the baby's in danger again."

Abby nodded, reassured because the doctor obviously assumed she would stay pregnant.

"Do you want someone to sit with you until your parents come? You have half the staff at your door."

Abby smiled. "Work brings me here often."

"Will any of them do for company?"

"Thanks, but I have another call to make."

"I'll tell everyone you're all right. We'll give you a room and you'll let us care for you tonight."

Abby thought of Trey, upstairs helping his wife deliver their baby. She couldn't afford for her pregnancy to make the department gossip rounds. "Do you have to put me in the maternity ward?"

The doctor frowned. "No, but don't anticipate a miscarriage. Your baby is still an embryo, still protected by your pelvic bone. I'm not sure why you were sick, unless the stress of the fight brought it on, but your baby should be safe." She made a final note. "I wouldn't engage in any more boxing matches. I noticed that bruise on your elbow. It didn't happen tonight?"

"Yesterday. But I hardly ever see trouble like this." She felt a bit more cheerful now that everything seemed to be okay.

"Good. As your pregnancy advances, you'll want to do that less and less."

Abby appreciated her pragmatism. "Okay." She

meant it. Nothing else would endanger her child if she had to ride a desk for the next thirty-six weeks.

"Make your call and we'll arrange for a room on a general floor. I'll make sure your parents find you."

"Thanks, but could I ask one more favor?"

"Sure." The doctor set Abby's chart on the table beside the ultrasound machine.

"Could you pass me my uniform? My cell phone is in the pocket." She had to warn Thomas she wouldn't be home after her shift.

Dr. Clegner passed the tidy stack of clothing Abby had folded to distract herself. But the pile felt light. She must have left her phone in the car or at the station. "It's not here."

"That's okay." The doctor pointed to the phone Abby had already used. "The call's on us."

She dialed, but this task drained her last semblance of composure. The moment she spoke, Thomas cut in.

"Where the hell are you?"

Had someone else called him? "At the emergency room," she said. "But it's nothing. My ribs— I had another fight tonight."

"Abby, tell me exactly what happened."

She explained the bar fight, mystified at his intensity. "What are you looking for?"

"A man called about an hour ago. I let the machine answer, and the guy told you to get out of this house before someone killed you."

Abby stared at her watch. Harv's warnings repeated in her head. If he was right, the bad guys had acted quickly. "A man?"

"Are you sure the guys at the bar didn't stage the fight to get at you?"

"I'm positive. I wasn't even supposed to work."

"That's true. Stay there. I'll bring the tape and come get you, and then we'll go to the station to report the threat."

Harv's words made more sense now, but understanding didn't frighten her. It made her mad as hell. "We can't report anything." She had to tell someone about Eddie Fontanero, but he obviously had friends who'd kept him safe so far.

"What are you talking about?"

"I'll explain when I see you, but don't call the police. I'm staying here tonight." A possible threat tempted her to tell him the truth about everything, but what could he do? After she told him about the baby, she couldn't take it back, and telling him on the spur of the moment would be irresponsible. "I'll come home in the morning."

"You're not staying alone in that hospital tonight."

"Mom and Dad are coming."

"You talked to your parents?"

"Why are you surprised?" She took a belligerent tone to remind him she had no reason to call him first.

It worked. He paused before he answered. "You

didn't have to worry them. I owe you for your help. I would have come."

"Thanks." Nothing more seductive than a man's sense of obligation. Her baby deserved love, not forced attention. "I'll see you tomorrow."

"Okay." But he obviously didn't like it. He was used to making the plans. "Tomorrow."

She'd been right to keep her secret. If he'd really cared for her, he couldn't have forced himself to stay home. In his place, she'd already be on her way to the hospital. She'd have needed to touch him to know he was safe.

"Good night," she said as someone thudded into her door, opening it. She hung up the phone in time to hold out her arms to her mom, who rushed into the room, clearly too frozen with fear to cry.

Elaine enveloped her in a hug that comforted Abby more than anything the hospital staff had done for her. Instead of crying again, she wrapped her arms around her mom's neck and clung.

"Thanks, Mother."

"We'll keep you safe."

"Elaine, make room, honey."

Abby laughed as her father joined the family embrace. They'd have plenty to say later about an intelligent woman who let herself get pregnant, but for now, their solace was good medicine.

Her mom leaned back far enough to find Abby's gaze. "Have you called Thomas?"

ABBY'S HOUSE FELT EMPTY without her. Sleep appeared to be a lost cause. Thomas checked his watch for maybe the fiftieth time, but only the second hand seemed to move.

He wandered to the kitchen and poured a glass of milk. Then he stared at the answering machine beside the phone. If he couldn't talk to Abby, maybe he could work on the message.

He punched a button to replay it. "Get out of that house, out of town, out of my way."

Thomas turned up the volume control. The rough voice might be a woman's. Or maybe Janie's strange behavior had him distracted. She'd be his first suspect.

He listened several more times. He'd never let someone tell him not to take action before. Sitting still for Abby's "I'll explain tomorrow" was completely out of character, but how could he push her harder when he had no idea how serious her injury might be?

He stared at the machine again. What if whoever had made that call knew Abby was in the hospital?

Thomas swore. What an idiot. He should have called the police, and he shouldn't have left Abby defenseless in a hospital room. If her parents had stayed, they'd just have to accept him.

Thomas ran upstairs. He changed into jeans and a sweater and grabbed his keys. The hospital's name had shown up on the Caller ID.

A quick computer search gave him the address.

Fifteen minutes later he persuaded the late-night information receptionist to give him Abby's room number. She thought she was giving it to a fiancé who'd flown in from out of town.

In case the rest of the hospital employees weren't as easily taken in, he crept up to Abby's room, completely out of bounds. Let someone try to remove him.

He shut her door at his back. A wall, presumably for her bathroom, obscured the head of her bed. Thomas eased around it. No parents.

The sight of Abby, asleep in bed, took him back to the first days after the bombing. When he'd prayed he might wake up to find one of his friends in the hospital with him.

His heart raced, out of control with the panic that had become his shameful friend. Just when he'd thought he was getting better. When would he be able to count on staying sane?

Abby took a deep breath. Thomas realized he'd been holding his own. He exhaled, relieved and self-conscious.

She rolled onto her side. Normally so full of life, she looked smaller than she was beneath a cocoon of blankets. He searched the ceiling for air vents. The dim room, its pale green walls lit only by a night-light beside a hotel-type dresser, was about the temperature of a slightly warming glacier.

He was almost annoyed she could sleep when he'd warned her someone was threatening her.

He lifted a chair and carried it to her side, trying to make no noise. He sat where he could see the door and Abby and the wide window that overlooked a sign for a local steakhouse.

Perfect. Someone had to keep watch.

"Thomas."

Despite being absolutely alert, he jumped and then laughed at himself.

Abby smiled, too. "What are you doing here?"

"I couldn't leave you alone."

Frowning, she tried to rise, but he put his hand on her shoulder to keep her still. "You didn't call the police?" she asked.

"No, but that's why I thought you might need someone who knew what was going on. Go back to sleep. I'll keep an eye out."

"You shouldn't. It's not good for me." Nevertheless, she pulled his hand from her shoulder and tucked it between hers beneath her chin. Almost immediately, she was asleep.

In the morning he'd find out why she didn't want him to look after her. For tonight, he balanced his arm between the chair, the rail on Abby's bed and her mattress, and quickly lost all sense of feeling. Just as well. Warm breath seeped from Abby's mouth across his skin. His body couldn't help responding.

He meant to stay awake, didn't realize he'd fallen asleep until he woke to find Abby staring at him. She released his hand, and he pulled it back, rubbing it to restore circulation.

"Sorry," he said, wishing she'd let him hold her. Since that night, she'd made their hands-off relationship very clear. "Some guard."

"We survived the night." She sat up. "And I'm hungry."

"Where did your parents go? I half thought they'd be here."

"Dad has a class this morning, and Mom was so worried we persuaded her they should both go home for a break." She tucked the blanket around her legs. "I needed a break, too."

"Explain about the phone call, Abby."

"The phone?" She pushed her hair out of her face, but it fell forward again. Sexy with sleep, she blinded him to anything but the need for her he kept trying to control. She didn't seem to recognize his change of heart. "Oh, that guy who called." She peered around the wall. "Is the door open?"

"I closed it."

"The guy who started the bar fight last night claimed he witnessed a murder. He said if someone else found out I knew, I'd be in danger, too." She smiled as if she felt silly saying the words. He loved the sweet curve of her mouth, hated seeing her in a hospital bed. He'd better get his mind back on business. "It sounds kind of crazy this morning," she said, "but you're living in my house, so you might be in trouble, too."

"You believed him?"

"More now, after the call." She swung her legs over the side of the bed and waited.

"What's wrong?" Thomas asked.

"I'm taking stock." She pressed her hand to her stomach, beneath her ribs. "Everything feels in order. I don't know if I believe Harv, but do you remember my friend, Catherine?"

"I remember the name."

"The M.E. determined that her husband, Jordan, died of a heart attack, but the circumstances were exactly as Harv described this murder. And he seemed to think if people could kill Jordan, they'd be happy to kill him." She looked at Thomas as if asking what he thought.

"Why would someone want to kill Jordan Tanner?"

"He was managing editor of the *Houston Sentinel,* and she's the Chief of Police now. Harv mentioned a cop who has a bad reputation. I'm wondering if Jordan planned an article on corruption, maybe. On the police force."

Dread tugged low in Thomas's gut. He wasn't about to let someone take potshots at Abby. Suddenly, Janie looked a lot less dangerous.

"I promised I'd meet Harv this morning."

"No." He couldn't help himself, but Abby laughed.

"Yes. As soon as I dress." She took tentative steps toward the built-in wood-veneer wardrobe and then opened the near door. "My uniform. Just what I need." She eased toward the bathroom. "You can go home."

"If you're determined to go, I'll come with you."

"Thomas, you're not a cop."

"You don't have to sound so gentle, as if you're reminding me, but I might be too out of my mind to know the difference."

"Sorry." She crooked a grin again. "You can't come along."

"I'm as stubborn as you." He crossed his legs, intimating he'd wait and watch as long as she forced him. "You might as well give in."

Her eyes narrowed. "No. This is my job. I'll do it. You wouldn't let me interfere with yours."

She took her clothes into the bathroom to change and he stared at the door, frustrated. She was right, damn it.

Abby dressed a lot quicker than he remembered. Within a few minutes, she came back, pulling her hair into a bunch on her head with mysterious hand motions.

"It's eight-forty. I need to hurry." She opened the door and peered into the hall. "Dr. Clegner." She leaned back in to glance at him. "I'll be right back, Thomas."

He was about to get fed up with having no choice. He gathered her things. She didn't have much, a purse and some keys. She'd left her shoes on the floor beside the bed.

They could use a spit polish.

The door opened and Abby returned. "I can check out downstairs. And would you believe I talked them out of a wheelchair?"

"Yeah, I believe."

"Time to go." She pushed her feet into her shoes. "Don't look so upset. I don't need a bodyguard."

He cared about her. Maybe she didn't want him in her life, but he knew she felt something for him. He let her glimpse affection he'd be wiser to control. "I know you can take care of yourself, but you have to stop doing crazy stuff."

"I'm a cop." She blew him off. "We believe in self-defense."

"You're just bad at it?"

She reached for her jacket with a rueful look. "That's funny, Thomas. My ribs can barely take the laughter."

He took the jacket and lifted it so she could slide her arms into the sleeves, slowly, as if the motion caused her pain. "You could shut me up if you'd take better care of yourself."

As she straightened her collar, her steady gaze challenged him—but why? "From now on, I'm vigilant about my safety."

He smoothed the jacket over her shoulders, stroking the leather when he'd rather caress her. The woman talked in riddles he couldn't solve, but he'd swear she'd just slapped him in the face with a message.

CHAPTER ELEVEN

DOWNSTAIRS, AT ABBY'S CAR, Thomas made a last effort. "Let me come with you."

"Calm down." She sounded like a soothing mom, which annoyed him more. "I'm meeting him at a café. He won't like seeing anyone with me, but no one else knows we're going there. Harv wouldn't tell anyone."

"He'll get used to me."

"Drop it, Thomas. Pretty soon, you'll go back to North Carolina, and I'll live on here, without your watchful eye."

"What are you? A glutton for punishment? Did this guy hit you last night?"

She shoved her key in the driver's door lock with a hint of impatience. "I don't know who hit me."

She took the physical abuse of her job too much in stride. "How about if I wait in the car?"

"Are you crazy?" Exasperation powered the deep breath she took. "What's the matter with you?"

"You are. I don't even know what happened to you last night."

"You don't always know—" She stopped. "Forget it. I've had enough of these go-nowhere skirmishes with you. Go home, and remember, we're friends, nothing more."

It was like being slapped again. She climbed into the car, her movements slow and sore. He'd like five seconds with the guy who could do that to Abby.

After two years in the desert, the cool air felt frosty. He hunched into his sweater and went to his own car.

For a long second he considered following her. He would have before. She'd have been angry, but she'd have forgiven him.

No wonder she'd left him in North Carolina. He'd never given her credit for being able to take care of herself.

He started the rental car, but the air was blue with his swearing by the time he turned out of the hospital parking lot.

He might have been swearing at himself. He'd smothered and then neglected a good, independent woman with strength that equaled his.

ABBY SLID INTO THE BOOTH across from Harv. Rumpled and bearded, he smelled less than delicate, but he looked sober.

"Coffee?" he asked.

"No, thanks." She looked longingly at his half-empty cup. "You go ahead."

"I will. I wasn't sure you'd come."

"I promised."

"You always keep your promises?"

"Always." She paused to ask for a bowl of oatmeal and a glass of orange juice. When their server walked away, she turned back to Harv. "What do you want to tell me today?"

Harv stared at her. "I hardly remember, myself."

Abby sighed. "Good thing I didn't tell anyone, huh?" She wasn't sure which Harv to believe, the drunk, desperate guy last night, or the stooped, stocky man with a hangover and second thoughts this morning.

"I had some money. I drank too much. I don't know what comes over me. It's a nightmare."

"I almost believed you."

"My parents died when I was six years old. In a house fire, but I lived. Ever since then I have had vivid nightmares, and they seem so real I remember the heat, the smell. My parents' screams. If I tip a few too many, I start believing the dreams are real."

"You dreamed what you told me?"

"I guess I tell them pretty well."

"Why do you drink, Harv?"

"Like I say, those dreams are more real than the real world sometimes."

"Would you think about treatment? I can get you into a place that might help you clean up."

"I'll think about it." He started to stand.

Abby grabbed Harv's sleeve. "Wait," she said. "What about the fact that your story sounds so much like the way Jordan Tanner died? Why are you dreaming of a stranger?"

"I read about it in his paper and everyone else's. He probably filtered into my nightmares." He pulled, trying to leave. "Forget it."

"And that other guy you mentioned? The one in the bar?"

"You know how many cops have picked me up over the years? He ended up in an appropriate role in my dream."

"You're talking a big coincidence."

"I don't know what to tell you," Harv said. "You've heard my story. This is what people will believe."

"I guess you have experience in trying to make people believe." Abby handed him another card. "You know where to find me if you change your mind," she said.

"Yeah."

And he bolted, a scared, thick-bodied mouse looking for a hole to hide in. Abby went to her car, but waited till he jumped on a bus at the next corner. No one followed him.

"WHAT DO YOU MEAN HE'S LYING?" Thomas smeared cream cheese over one of the bagels Abby had brought home. "Today? Or last night?"

"Today. Funny how a lie makes you believe a guy's doubtful story."

"A threat on your answering machine helps. What are you going to do now?"

"I have to talk to Catherine." She closed her eyes, tired and reluctant.

"I'll come with you."

"No." Her tone warned him another argument was futile. "We haven't really talked since Risa's investigation. I can't tell her I think her husband was murdered while you stand by. She doesn't know you, and this is going to be hard enough without explaining you're the guy I put ahead of my career."

He tried to see her side. "She won't give a damn who I am, but if you believe Harv, you have to believe the police are involved. They wouldn't have sent the crooked cop after him."

"I'm not worried in the station." She took a bite of her own bagel. "Why didn't the M.E. find evidence? I have to talk to Catherine before Harv or anyone else gets killed."

"Abby, you have circles under your eyes. Your lips have no color." He went to the fridge and brought her a bottle of water.

"Thanks."

"You need to rest."

She agreed with a nod of her head. "But I have to talk to Catherine first. She goes to the office on most Saturdays, and I worked out of that building last night. I think I left my phone in the car so I have a reason to be there."

Thomas wanted to pull her into the safety of his arms. The heck with chauvinism. He couldn't bear the thought of someone hurting her. "If you're worried about how you look to your colleagues, you believe Harv."

"I don't want to make an appointment with Catherine that could be traced." She sipped her water. "I'll drop in on her. People know we've been friends."

"Maybe Catherine will agree with Harv's new story. Her husband died of natural causes and Harv's drinking problem is out of hand."

"I don't think that's going to happen."

"Why are you so willing to believe your fellow cops might be up to murder?"

"I'm not. But Eddie means shady business," she said. "I hear rumors. More than that, Harv's scared gutless. A man that panicked has reason."

FROM THE SECOND she entered the lobby, Abby regarded everyone through a confused haze of suspicion. All because of a guy who admitted he drank until he suffered delusions.

She stopped to ask the watch commander if anyone had turned in her cell phone, but before she reached his desk, two familiar women turned and came around it.

"Risa, Crista." Abby hardly believed her eyes. Risa and Crista must have completed that work they'd started on their differences.

The other women looked up from their conversation. Both detectives, dressed in neat, professional-looking suits, they made Abby conscious of her not-so-neat uniform. Crista, beautiful and dark, opened her arms with affection that hadn't always come easily to her. She'd lived a hard life in a rough Houston neighborhood, and her response had been self-defense first.

"Abby, I'm glad you're all right." Her black hair swept over one shoulder as she stepped back. "Risa has your phone."

Risa beckoned Abby out of the foot traffic, to one side of the hall. She held up the cell phone.

"I came down to meet Crista for lunch and ask the watch commander about an arrest one of the officer's made yesterday, and he asked me if I might see you."

"He told us about the bar fight." Crista's shrewd gaze swept Abby.

"Said you had to stay overnight in the hospital," Risa said.

"Thanks." Taking the phone, Abby felt heat on her face. She'd rather not explain her hospital stay. The moment grew stilted. They only met by accident lately.

Crista cut through the awkwardness. "I'm glad you came to pick up the phone, too. Come to lunch with us."

"I can't. I have an errand here, and then…" Then she had to go home and report to Thomas before he sent her own department searching for her.

"He's still there?" Risa asked.

"Who?" Crista looked curious. For a second it felt like the old days.

"Thomas." Abby started to take a defensive stand, but Crista smiled. "You're talking again? I'm glad. You have to deal with the past or it keeps coming back to you."

"You're glad?" Risa clearly wasn't. "She needs to get this guy out of her life before he hurts her again."

"Crista, I heard you and Alex Del Rio are together." Abby thought she might as well turn the spotlight onto someone else.

Crista's happy smile startled her. She looked different, content from within. Alex headed the mayor's task force, and Crista had met him while investigating a series of drive-by shootings in which his young daughter had been wounded. "I'm good," Crista said. "Happy."

"You look it." Abby hesitated. "Look, guys, I need to talk to you." She grinned at Risa. "Not about Thomas."

"What's wrong?" Crista was instantly concerned, as if their friendship had never ruptured.

Mindful that she needed to reach Catherine, Abby waffled. "I don't have time to go far."

Risa pointed at the door marked Stairs, about five

feet down the busy hall. With an appreciative nod, Abby led the way.

Risa shut the door once they were inside the stairwell. "What's up?"

Before answering, Abby made sure they were alone, checking both up the stairs and down, listening for footsteps. "It's kind of a work question." She almost asked if they'd keep her confidences quiet, but then realized she didn't have to.

"Is this why you look so distressed?" Crista leaned against the door to keep it closed. "I hope we can help."

Abby smiled, acknowledging her bad grooming. "I arrested a guy last night, and he told me this story about a murder he witnessed. Today, he says it's an alcoholic nightmare, but I'm not sure. It sounds like a case I heard of."

They waited for her to explain.

She couldn't explain the rest of Harv's story in case it put them in danger, but she got to the point. "Have you heard anything questionable about the department? I'm talking irregularities."

Crista's expression was blank. "I've heard rumors. And after uncovering corruption in my department nothing would surprise me."

"I've heard rumors, too," Risa said. "Probably the same ones you have about the same people, but nothing I'm comfortable stating as fact."

Abby nodded. "I understand. Same here, until

this. The guy I talked to is concerned that cops were involved in this killing."

Crista's frown deepened. "What will you do?"

"Talk to the people closest to the victim."

"What if this guy's wrong?" Risa asked. "You might raise some painful questions for no reason."

Abby took a deep breath. "Good point."

"You can't ignore it," Crista said.

"This person's been dead a year, and I believe my witness."

"No proof?"

"None." If only Harv had managed to keep that drink bottle. "Except his story is plausible. His drinking problem's worse because of what he saw."

"Why didn't he speak up?"

"He tried, but then he discovered the cops might be in on it."

"And you think he might be right?"

"I wonder." She didn't mention the threat on her answering machine. She wanted to hear it before she talked about it.

"You can't let a killer go free," Risa said. "Who else might have died?"

"Or might still?" Abby asked by way of agreement.

Crista put out one hand. "Can we help?"

Abby had spoken because they knew Catherine, but she couldn't mention their other friend. "Thanks, no. I just wanted to hear what you'd do if you had this problem."

"Talk to the family." Crista looked certain as she smiled at both her friends. "Imagine how you'd feel. I spent a long time avoiding everything that made me who I am, but if there was the slightest possibility someone had hurt my family, I'd want to know."

"That's true." Suddenly, Abby dreaded talking to Catherine, but no longer doubted that she should. She tucked her phone into her pocket and loosely wrapped her arms around both women. "I hate to be rude, but I have to go. Thanks for the advice."

"Be careful, Abby." Risa stepped back with Crista. "On both counts. Thomas and this other guy."

Crista shook her head. "Abby knows how to take care of herself." Her kind smile reached out to Abby in a sweet reminder of their old friendship.

"I'm trying to keep from being noticed," Abby said. "But I'm so glad I saw you both."

Crista opened the door to the floor again. "Let's meet for drinks."

Abby was happy to agree. One more non-alcoholic drink to explain. "I need to talk to you all like this more often." She started up the stairs. "I go this way."

"Call me," Risa said.

"Okay."

The door closed behind both women, and Abby made a private trek to Catherine's office. On the right floor, she opened the door slowly and then leaned around it to make sure she met no one else.

Light shone from the Chief of Police's office, but her secretary hadn't joined her on a workaholic's Saturday.

Abby hurried to the open door and knocked. "Catherine?" She cleared her throat. "I mean, Chief?"

Catherine looked up, surprise in her eyes. "Abby."

"Do you have a few minutes?"

She tucked straight blond hair behind one ear, looking reluctant. "Is this personal or professional?"

"I haven't forgotten the chain of command if that's what you mean." Abby slipped inside the door and closed it. "But the answer is, I don't know."

Catherine Tanner straightened, setting her pen beside the file in front of her. Even seated, she was taller than most women, forceful. "What's happened?"

"Now that I'm here, I don't know how to tell you." She'd come to relate exactly the same news she'd dreaded hearing about Thomas all those years ago. News she still never wanted to hear. "It's about Jordan."

Catherine looked as if she'd prefer not to listen. "Go on."

"It's bad."

"Go on, I said."

Her inner steel reassured Abby. She related last night's call at the bar and Harv's stories. Both of them. Catherine also doubted his morning-after explanation.

"Have you checked his story about his parents?"

"No, but I will."

"You think he was telling the truth last night?"

At Catherine's mix of dread and anger, Abby wanted to hug the Chief of Police. Once, they would have comforted each other. "I'm afraid I do, Catherine. He's either sick or honest, more likely both."

Catherine held her silence with a tight mouth. She didn't even mention Fontanero. To do so would have been inappropriate. "Can you reach this Stuckey?"

"Yes, but I have to tell you one more thing. I had a phone call last night. Someone left a message that I should get out of the way. I haven't been doing anything else that would put me in someone's way. At the least, it's coincidental, so soon after I spoke with Harv."

Catherine picked up a pen. "On second thought, don't reach him. Give me his information, and I'll take over from here. If he's right, you and he may be in danger. If he's wrong, I want to know."

"I wish I could have done anything else with this information."

"I'm all right." Catherine stood. Her eyes glittered suspiciously, as if moisture had pooled in them, but her nearly frozen face repelled any attempt at solace.

Abby turned to the door again. Unspoken words colored the air between them. The prickly silence of a friendship gone awry, but well missed. "If I can help, call me."

"Abby?"

She paused, her hand on the knob, and looked back. Catherine looked slightly less grim.

"Have you heard from the others lately? Risa or Lucy or Crista or Mei Lu?"

"I spoke to Crista and Risa earlier. It was good." Abby sounded a bit wistful even to herself. "Risa seems happy with Grady. I really haven't talked to Mei Lu or Lucy enough to know what's going on with them." She didn't mind exposing her regret.

Catherine rubbed her face. "Thanks for bringing this to me. I have to decide what to do."

"I'm worried about Harv."

"I'll make sure he's all right."

Despite her brave words, Catherine's bleak gaze touched Abby. "Can I do anything for you, Catherine?"

"Not now." She stacked the papers from her file, pulling back now that she'd exposed her emotions. "Thanks for coming."

Abby nodded and left the office. Working for Catherine made rapprochement even more difficult.

THOMAS WENT FOR A RUN while he waited for Abby to come home this time. Physical action made him feel more like a man, less as if he was holding her purse while she took care of business.

After his run, he took the paper outside and read it on the front porch. He felt a little guilty for resenting Abby when she finally drove up, her smile absent.

"You talked to Catherine?"

"I don't know how much good I did, but I told her and she asked me to let her take care of it from here."

He dropped the paper into his lap. "You trust her?"

Abby nodded, slumping into the chair across from his. "No question."

"You look exhausted. How are your ribs?"

"Fine." But her glance skittered from his as if he'd asked for the combination to her gun locker. She picked up his coffee cup and the coolish breeze pushed her scent across the table to him.

God, she smelled good, like every dream he'd had of her in the past six years. He'd never forget the scent of Abby on his skin if he never saw her again. That thought sat uneasily on his mind.

Not see Abby again?

"Can I get you a cup?" he asked. "You look as if you could use a jolt of caffeine."

"I didn't stop for makeup before I went to the hospital."

He studied her brown hair and dark eyes, her pale skin normally warmed with the life that powered Abby's will to defend all needy victims. "I just meant you look tired."

"I am."

"Then should I get you that coffee?"

"I'm dreaming of a glass of cold grape juice," she said.

Whatever. He was grateful to do anything for her. He poured a glass in the kitchen and added some melon and strawberries on a small plate. She loved fresh fruit.

Back on the porch he found Abby had fallen asleep. He eased the plate onto the table, and she opened her eyes with reluctance, but she smiled as if she didn't mind seeing him.

He cradled her chin with his fingers. Did she realize she looked at him as if she needed him?

"No," she said with a start as if she'd suddenly come to, and realized he was about to kiss her.

"No?" Kneeling, he brushed his lips against hers, wanting her, but more acutely craving the reassurance that she was real, not another dream in the desert of his life without her.

"Thomas?"

He lifted his head and looked into her eyes again. "Sorry. I needed that. Badly."

She shook her head. "Don't say or do anything we can't take back."

"Isn't it too late for that? Eventually, we have to talk about what happened between us the night we made love."

"I don't see why."

The hard porch was cold beneath his knees, and the cold crept upward. "It mattered to me, Abby."

"And to me." She pressed the back of one hand to his cheek. Wrapping her arms around his neck, she pulled him down to her.

She opened her mouth beneath his and he gave himself up to the longing he felt in her touch, her mouth, the pressure of her palm on his neck.

The arm of her chair bit into his stomach. Abby breathed in gasps, as if she was about to cry, and he pulled her as close as he could bring her. She buried her face in his chest. Somewhere a wind chime sang. Branches from a small shrub rubbed the side of the porch. Thomas tugged the elastic band from Abby's hair and slid his fingers into the strands, holding her head against him.

Truth was, he couldn't get close enough to Abby.

CHAPTER TWELVE

LATER THAT AFTERNOON, Abby and Thomas went to the grocery store like any two people who shared a house. Abby had started on her own, but there was no leaving Thomas behind this time.

She didn't care for the feel of couple-shopping. Or maybe she liked it too much. As they shook their heads simultaneously at pineapple cream cheese and Thomas put it back on the shelf, Abby thought she'd be wise to run. Only a madwoman bonded in the dairy aisle with a man she didn't intend to know soon.

Back in the car, with Thomas driving, Abby put her head back. She was trying not to talk, because she didn't trust herself not to blurt out baby news at any moment—but she fell asleep.

She woke as Thomas slowed the car. Her head had rolled toward him on the rest. "What?" she asked, still fuzzy with sleep.

He pulled to the side, and a police car sped past, lights whirling. Thomas rested his hand on her wrist as if to reassure her. She wanted to pull her hand away, but the moments she had left with him were so few.

"It's all right." He smiled, his mouth hard and masculine and too disturbing to ignore.

Alarms clanged in her head. He'd taken that kiss on her porch seriously. The child she could not share with him meant she had to be smarter than she ever had been with Thomas. She dragged free of his intense gaze, and her brain began to function. "Maybe I'm starting to get paranoid, but did you notice that police car's headed for my house?"

Thomas turned to watch the disappearing lights. Without a word, he hit the gas and sped after it. As they drew closer, Abby saw she'd been right.

Her front door was wide open and Ken Paymer, another patrol officer, was entering, his gun drawn. The second Thomas parked, Abby launched herself from the car. Thomas got in front of her as she hurried up the walkway.

At the porch, Thomas stopped and Ken caught her, but they all stared at the spray-painted lettering on the front of her house.

"They aren't loving," Ken said, "but I've seen worse."

The words repeated the message from last night. Get Out Of This House and Get Out Of Town; finally, Get Out Of My Way. But they were nothing that seemed as serious as a plan to kill the police chief's husband.

"Herb." Abby pushed past Ken, into the hall. The cat wouldn't answer her call if she ran at his heels, sporting a gigantic catnip mouse.

She took the stairs as fast as she could go. Thomas came behind her.

"Let me go first," he said.

"Abby, I haven't checked the house," Ken called from below.

"Whoever wrote that isn't violent," she said. "Check downstairs for my cat, and we'll do up here."

Thomas broke off at his room. Abby checked the bathrooms and the closets quickly. No Herb and no burglars, either. "Kitty, kitty?" She was half under her bed, shifting shoes and storage boxes when Thomas spoke in a soothing tone.

She scooted out, blowing dust bunnies off her face, and nearly burst into tears at the sight of Herb, hissing in Thomas's arms.

"Hiding under my bed," Thomas said as the cat struggled to reach the top of his head. "Tell Ken I'm locking him in the bathroom up here. I don't think whoever it was got this far. The alarm must have scared him off."

"Let me hold him." She clutched her cat with relief, ignoring Thomas's indulgent smile to press her face in Herb's dusty fur. She clearly didn't clean often enough under her beds.

Herb struggled for freedom. Thomas took pity on him and eased him out of Abby's arms.

"He's all right. Let's put him in the bathroom so he can't run out. You should get back to your friend downstairs. He's sounding peeved."

"Okay." She wiped her eyes. She was turning into the worst crybaby. Must be her baby dancing on her hormones. Several deep breaths later, she started down the stairs.

Two more voices shouted her name in tandem from the bottom of the walkway. Abby's stomach spasmed as she glanced back at Thomas coming down the stairs. Her mother believed she should tell him about the baby. Her mother tended to be a loose cannon.

"Excuse me, Ken." She rushed past him to meet her parents. Her mom, hair unwashed, clothes a little rumpled, eyed her with an empty gaze. "Everything's fine," Abby said, her mind blank as she tried to think of a way to keep her mom away from Thomas. "I wasn't even home. How did you hear?"

"You know Vetta Sanders next door?" Abby's dad hugged her, staring at the painted words. "Since she retired she spends her time with her ear pressed to a police scanner. Don't ask me how she knew where you live, but she bellowed your address through the window and told us there'd been a break-in."

"And we came running." Elaine hugged her, too, trembling as she did when she was coming off her meds. "Are you all right?" She peered past Abby's shoulder, thankfully too busy searching for Thomas to notice the graffiti.

"Fine." Abby moved between her mother and Thomas, now deep in conversation with Ken. She glanced up and down the street, noting those of her neighbors who hadn't come to see the fun. Who might have seen her unwelcome visitor?

"Come stay with us tonight," her dad spoke up.

Abby glanced at her mom. Her father caught her hand.

"We'll work this out," he said. "I found the stash."

Every time her mother stopped taking her medication, a little pile of pills turned up somewhere. Abby looked at her houseguest again. "I can't."

"I'm here, John. I know when you're talking about me, and Abby, I don't think you need to worry I'll hurt that man," her mom said.

Abby could walk, fearless, into a bar filled with angry, fighting men, but taking Thomas to her parents' house would be plain reckless. "I don't think he'd come."

"You can't stay here tonight." Tears seeped out of Elaine's eyes. She'd have been surprised to find she was crying. Abby knew the signs. Her mom was holding on to her emotions like a woman gripping a lifeline. "Somebody's out to get you," Elaine said through gritted teeth.

"Mother."

"Come," her father said. "I've already persuaded

your mother to take the medicine she skipped this morning."

"I had to take it or he wouldn't bring me, Abby. I just wanted to make sure my baby was okay. You understand that?"

"Mom." She said the word in panic. If Thomas heard…

"Come with us and I'll change your locks tomorrow," her dad said. "I don't want you to stay here, either. Why would someone do this?"

"Someone's out to get her. Can't you hear me, John?"

"I hear you, honey." He held Abby's mom close to his side.

"Dad, I can't." Abby felt helpless. She didn't dare risk letting her mom tell Thomas about the baby, but she didn't want to worry her parents, either. "I'll do the locks tonight."

"Ease our minds, Abby. You'll want a meal and a soft bed. Stay with us." Her dad made the suggestion sensible. "We won't hurt the man, and I'll make sure nothing bad happens."

Her mom wouldn't mean to hurt their grandchild's father, but she was easing into the grip of the manic, fevered emotions that always led to days in a dark room.

"Mom, why did you—"

"Abby," her dad cut in, "she just wants to be normal."

"Hello? I have ears." Her mother broke away from them and went to Thomas. "You'll bring our girl to stay with us tonight, won't you?"

He looked over her head at Abby, his compassion almost unbearable. "We can do whatever makes you comfortable, Mrs. Carlton."

Abby didn't want memories of Thomas under the roof of her family's home. Innocuous threats didn't scare her, but they might not be the extent of the danger. Maybe leaving the house alone and alarmed in case anyone came back tonight would be a good idea.

Her dad turned her mom toward their car. "We'll get back. Things'll be fine, Abby. You'll see."

Abby nodded, strangely alone. Her father was caught in the same hard place that trapped her. He didn't want to hurt her mom, but he didn't want his child hurt, either. Abby had always taken care of her mom, but now her child was her first concern, and having Thomas find out anything she wasn't ready to tell him terrified her.

She climbed the porch steps slowly. Ken and Thomas made room for her in their huddle. "Your friend here suggested someone was testing the alarm," Ken said.

"To see how long it took the police or the alarm service to show up." Thomas shrugged. "He might have been trying to see if the police came, rather than the company."

Abby focused on her house rather than her secrets. "It might be a prank. Kids in the neighborhood going too far."

Ken turned to the painting again. "I agree it doesn't look too serious. Let's say a burglar wanted to know if anyone cared if he broke in and stole Abby's valuables—"

"Assuming I had any."

Ken smiled. "He knows we'll be here before he can take them."

"Why assume it's a man?" Abby asked.

"The door's broken." Thomas pointed to the shattered wood around the plate on the doorframe. "Someone with a strong will wanted inside."

"A woman with a crowbar, for instance?" She couldn't let him bring up Harv's story until Catherine was ready to have it come out.

"I get it, Abby." He looked extremely unhappy, his mouth sealed in a straight, stern line.

"I don't. You have some other ideas?" Ken asked.

"No." Abby said it before Thomas could be tempted to protect her.

"I guess we can't do much here. You hardly had any damage. No one took anything." Ken glanced at Abby. "Those people were your mom and dad?"

"Yeah."

"You're staying with them tonight?"

"You know how parents are." She eyed Thomas.

"I'd like to change the locks and reset the alarm code first."

"Good idea," Ken said. "If you find the guy stole something, let me know." He pounded her on the back, ignoring her flinch. "You know how this works."

"For today, I'll take care of the locks and pack up my cat."

"I'll see you around, then." And Ken donned his hat, shook hands with Thomas and left, lights and siren quiet as he parted her neighbors.

"I can go to a hotel," Thomas said.

"Don't. I want you to come. And I'd worry about you if you stayed here." She sounded like an echo of her mom.

"Would you?" His surprise, in a husky voice, teased her sensitized nerve endings. "Worry about me?"

She stared, breathing through her mouth because she couldn't seem to take in enough air. "I need the carrier."

"For Herb?"

She nodded. "It's in the garage. Could you get it while I run to the hardware store?"

"Sure. We can't leave your most precious possession behind."

"What kind of a cop would you make?" Abby teased him, but avoided looking straight at him. "No one owns Herb."

THOMAS COULDN'T FIND a minute alone with Abby. Her parents clung to her side all night, as if they were afraid he'd attack or something. Her mother alternated between whirring around the house at top speed and suddenly subsiding in unnatural stillness to watch Abby as if she expected doom.

They ate a somber dinner he'd never remember if someone administered Sodium Pentothal to drag a description out of him. Abby and her father watched her mom as if she might explode at any second. Thomas felt bad for Elaine. Claiming he was tired at an ungodly early hour, he climbed the stairs to get out of the family's hair.

He lay on his borrowed bed for hours, but as soon as the Carltons quieted, he locked his door and climbed out the window. A wraparound porch gave access to Abby's window, and he knocked on the frame.

He had to knock three times before the lamp flickered on behind lace curtains. After a few seconds, she came to the window and a scowl replaced sleepy curiosity. "What?" she mouthed.

He motioned to her to unlock and open the window. She actually considered refusing. What the hell went on beneath the tension around here? He felt as if he were clinging to a window ledge in a spotlight, rather than waiting on a perfectly comfortable porch in the early part of a cold, Houston night.

The window stuck, but Abby managed to open

it. "Imagine what my mother will do if she finds you in here."

"Give the woman a break and go lock your door." He forgot to whisper.

She cringed. "Keep it down, Thomas."

"Make sure your mom can't walk in. I already locked my door."

She hurried across the room, flipped the old-fashioned lock and came back. "What do you want?"

"We need to talk about the burglary that wasn't."

"Is that all?" She reached for the screen. "I don't know how this comes off."

"Metal catches at the corners. You'll need a chair for the top two."

With further low-voiced assistance, she unlatched the screen and he pulled it off and then immediately slid over the sill. Abby backed away.

"Ken's right. It's not serious enough to worry about."

"You and I know more about it than you told Ken. You should have told him about the phone threat and Harv."

"I told Catherine, and she asked me not to spread it around yet. I'll let her know about the break-in, but Jordan was her husband."

"She gets first shot at revenge?" He smiled, startled that she understood the need to pay off a vendetta. "I thought you were a forgiveness-first girl."

Abby glanced back at her door as if she expected

her parents to bust it in. "Are you making fun of me?"

"No." She put her arms around herself, drawing his gaze to the short, tight T-shirt that barely skimmed the top of her loose pajama pants. The temperature in her room seemed to skyrocket. "You didn't come in here because of what I didn't tell Ken."

"No?" She might be right, but he wasn't in the mood to face his own motives. Some things hadn't changed. He could face that day in the desert and the firefight that had taught him he wasn't a perfect soldier, but he hadn't learned how to live with his new awareness. He couldn't tell Abby he needed her until he knew what to expect from himself.

"I won't make any more mistakes, and I'm not about to get involved with a commitment-shy man." She broke off as if she'd used her last breath. "You can't stay with me tonight."

"You know I could change your mind."

"But you're a decent man so you won't try."

He had to laugh. "Not fair, Abby."

"You have to fight with the weapons you have." She turned him. Her hands felt small on his shoulders, but he let her direct him back to the window. "Thomas?"

"Hmm?" He turned enough to meet her gaze. "You smell good."

"How much longer are you going to need Liam?"

"I don't know. You're ready for me to leave?" It shouldn't hurt this much.

"I didn't mean that." She hugged him from behind, and he knew she was lying. Her breasts against his back tempted him to turn, but she moved away.

"Liam and I argued yesterday. You're a bone of contention between us."

"He thinks I married him while I was still hoping you'd come after me."

"Did you?" He'd wanted to come, but he'd loved her too much to hurt her again. No one could be more wrong for Abby than he was. She needed stability, safety.

"I thought I loved him."

He flinched. "Why did you make love with me that night after I first talked to him?"

She lowered her head. Deep breaths lifted her breasts. "I don't know," she said, her voice so low he had to lean down to hear.

"Goodbye?" He'd always known, but deep down where he'd kept all his secrets from her before, he wished that she still wanted him in her life.

She looked up, determination firming her gaze. "I don't know, but right now I'm saying good-night."

He let her push him toward the window again. "We have to talk, Abby. I'm no more a love 'em and leave 'em type than you are."

She stopped, and he continued to the window.

"I thought that was exactly who you are."

Her quiet voice turned him around. "What?" He went back to her. "You left me. We were together for over a year. I wouldn't have left."

He'd have sworn tears glittered in her eyes, but the dim light made him unsure. He'd made too many assumptions about her already.

"What's the matter with you, Abby? Let me help you for a change."

Suddenly, she took a step closer. "I wish I knew you could help." Her sexy tone made him feel guilty for wanting her when she needed something more than lust.

"What's wrong? You know I'd do anything for you."

"How would I know that?" Startling him, she put her arms around his neck and sank against him.

Her impulsive, hungry kiss made him forget good intentions and kindness. He hauled her off the ground, pulling her tight against his body.

"Abby." He pressed his face into her thick, soft hair. "Let me stay."

"I can't." She reached for the floor and pushed him away, her hands shaking as she pressed them against his chest. "When you're all better, we'll talk about—everything." Still pushing at his chest, she urged him all the way to the window. "'Night, Thomas."

"I don't understand." Should he abide by her

wishes and let her shove him outside, or be a man and demand to know what she was talking about?

"Go, Thomas. Please." She bore down so hard he fell onto the sill.

Abby looked fierce, fight in her eyes like he'd never seen before. "Don't make me leave you like this."

"I want you to stay, but being together tonight would be wrong."

He did as she asked. He could be a man when he learned how to stand up to his own future.

HOURS LATER, Abby opened her window again and breathed in the cold air. *Stay,* had lingered so long on the tip of her tongue. *Stay, and let me tell you the truth* had tempted her.

How could she force so much responsibility on him? He'd do "the right thing." She'd never know if he did it out of love or necessity, and she didn't want him because he believed a strong man stepped up to the plate.

He hadn't asked to be a father. He might not want a child. He had to be healthy again before she'd ask him to decide.

She went back to her bed, lay down on her side and wrapped her arms around her belly. She fought her jumbled thoughts until too much sadness stilled her hunger for Thomas. At last, she slept.

But not for long. Morning came for her before

sunrise. She showered and changed and went downstairs to make breakfast for the others. She was watching the news over a glass of orange juice when her mom and dad came down. Thomas brought up the rear, wary after her behavior last night. Abby avoided him, turning off the small TV on the counter.

"Something smells good." From no makeup yesterday, her mom had switched to too much today. Her hair, clean now, was wild, unlike her more usual chignon. "What a treat. Thomas, how do you like your coffee?"

"Huh?" He turned to Elaine, startled at her brittle generosity.

Abby frowned, too. Her mother had always treated him like the head of an invading force, bent on spiriting her only child away.

"Your coffee?" Elaine asked again.

"Black." He watched her go to the cabinet and take down a cup and then fill it. "Thanks."

"Sure. What did you cook, Abby?" She sniffed the air in a gesture most unlike her ladylike self, and Abby worried what she'd do next.

"A casserole with eggs and cheese and everything else you had in the fridge. Not healthy, but comfort food for a cold day."

"What's up, Abby? You don't look so well." Her dad reached for the newspaper, but then dropped it, his expression sharpening. "Should we call a doctor?"

Abby slid away and stood, alarmed. Thomas was

no idiot. He wouldn't have to be if one of her parents spilled her baby news. "No. I'm going home."

Thomas and both her parents stared.

"My house is a mess." She had to break up this happy little faux family.

"I'm ready." Thomas emptied his cup into the sink. She could have thanked him for not insisting on breakfast.

Her mother's smile was too bright. "Why leave now?"

"I have a lot to do and I need to clean my uniforms. Tomorrow's a workday."

"It's barely morning yet," her mom said.

"If Abby wants to go, Elaine," her father said, "we shouldn't get in her way. You can hold a daughter too close."

"It's nothing like that, Mom. I just have all my weekend errands to do before a workday. Go ahead and eat, Thomas. I'll get my things."

They'd both brought a bag the night before. Abby repacked her pajamas and toothbrush and turned to find her mother standing in the middle of her room.

"You startled me, Mom."

"I wouldn't tell him without your permission."

Abby swept to the door and closed it. "Shh."

"He's eating. Has he been on a diet? He looks thinner, but he's found an appetite this morning."

"Mom, you and Dad can't drop hints like hand

grenades. If you're suddenly all friendly, and Dad talks about doctors, he's going to guess."

"He deserves to know." Elaine grabbed Abby's arms. Her eyes burned, and so did her cheeks, in two splotches of too much color. "Look at me," Elaine said. "Are your mistakes my fault?"

"Mom, calm down. Don't get overexcited."

"Stop." Elaine pushed her away. "I'm allowed feelings like everyone else. Don't assume I'm crazy. I'm the mother, Abby. Not you."

Had she usurped her mother's place? How could she not? Her mom had needed more care than Abby for most of her childhood. "I only tried to help." Her voice broke. "I wanted to be like the girls in my class at school, sharing makeup and clothes and—whatever girls share with a mother." Elaine began to cry and Abby tried to put her arms around her.

"No." Elaine broke free. "I can't change the past." Even though she looked as if she'd been nailed to it and couldn't escape her own guilt.

"I need you." Abby stood where she was. "I always do."

A sob broke between Elaine's lips. Abby wanted to disappear. "You assume you can't count on me."

"I see your face and I feel happy, Mom."

"Not at first." Her mother had been ill, not insensate. "Not until you're sure I'm on an even keel. I can't afford to be too up or too down with my own husband and daughter."

"I'm not sorry we try to take care of you—"

Elaine came back. "Let me care for you. I know you can't hide Thomas's child and live with yourself. Give him a chance. Think of your own father, how he'd have felt if things had been the same for us."

"Dad wanted me. You both planned for me." They'd planned everything back then—their careers, their future, their allotted two-point-five children, until pregnancy hormones and the onset of bipolar disease had changed the Carlton family forever.

"You can't plan everything," Elaine said, obviously reaping the pain of similar thoughts.

Abby turned to pick up her bag. "I'm protecting my child." She pushed her hair off her forehead. "Thomas didn't know I wasn't using birth control. This isn't his fault. And he's not in any shape to decide whether we share a baby."

"Your dad and I guessed something was wrong with him." Elaine caught her hand, forcing the bag to the floor. "Sick or not, Thomas has a right to know about his baby."

"My baby. My decision."

"And your child will be better off without her father?"

"Maybe. He was hurt in battle. You can see he's different."

"Kinder, more thoughtful. He's careful with you."

"I can't hold him to a decision he makes under duress." The problem was she couldn't know. "And he could change back."

"Fine. He has problems that may stay with him the rest of his life. He needs you more. He hides dark feelings that I assume he's shared with you, and that's why you're scared."

Abby nodded, thinking back to the night they'd made this baby.

"Would you have been better off if your father had left and taken you from me? Do you wish he'd protected you from my problems?"

CHAPTER THIRTEEN

THOMAS SAW JANIE before Abby as they turned onto her street. Janie swayed from side to side, clipping leaves off the live oak with her hand, and yet she seemed to be holding a furtive watch.

"Look." He pointed to a garbage can rolled onto its side on the opposite curb. "The wind must have come up last night."

"I see her. I was only trying to decide how to make you stop for her without arguing."

"Don't make me, Abby. She's obviously…"

"I know. I'll take her to Reverend Michael." She checked her watch. "Or somewhere. Last time he said he wouldn't take Janie in again in this shape."

He swallowed an urge to congratulate the good minister on his wise decision. "You could take her to jail. A night there might convince her she doesn't enjoy the life."

"You can be hard sometimes, Thomas."

"I'm just not soft." He stared straight ahead, absorbing his own self-revelation. He cared about people, but Janie, whom Abby had taken under her wing, was dangerous, using Abby, rather than the help she offered. "Stop?"

"No." She looked away as they passed. "I'll come back for her after you get out. She'll see you don't like her."

"She won't care what I think. Janie's disturbed and she depends on you too much. You're strapping Band-Aids over the problem because she doesn't want to stop drinking."

"How do you know?" She sounded riled.

He didn't blame her. He had no right, but he took off the gloves. "Getting her into a shelter or your house for the night keeps her warm and safe for an evening. She needs structured care. She needs to want it."

"She tries."

"She uses her alcoholism to stay close to you."

He expected her to jump down his throat. He'd be tempted. Instead, she stopped to consider.

"I can't shut the door on her. She needs help."

"And you need to be the one who helps."

"You're free with the diagnoses today." She sat up. "What happened to your appointment with Liam yesterday?"

Thomas had to laugh, aware the wisdom he was dispensing might be flawed. "I annoyed him so much he needed time off."

Abby's laugh made him feel everything might be right again. "That, I believe. You'd drive the world's best psychologist crazy." She pointed to her driveway. "Stop and I'll switch seats. Liam's coming today?"

"Unless he bails again."

"Every man's entitled to save his own sanity."

He parked and she swung out of the car. Still grinning at his expense, she came around the back and held out her hand for the keys.

"You know I'm right." He nodded toward Janie, shambling into view.

"Until I think of a better alternative, I have to help her."

"Give me time to call Liam. If he'll put off our session until afternoon, I'll come with you."

"She has feelings." She gestured for the keys again. "You've already made me hesitant with her."

"Good enough. I'll settle for your reluctance." He dropped the keys in her palm.

She took them and shot him a severe look as she slid behind the steering wheel. Backing out, she turned her face toward Janie and the back of her head on Thomas.

He headed up the walk to her door. Considering he'd climbed in her window and tried to make love to her without commitment and then offered her plans to improve her life this morning, he probably deserved worse.

"YOU HAVE NO ROOM?" Abby eyed Dr. Gatehouse, the Friendship Center's director with disbelief. "I have a sick woman. You receive public funds to help people like Janie, and you tell me you don't have room?"

"Are you accusing me of lying?" The man's haughty gaze felt too intense. His anger, stronger than made sense, bounced into Abby.

"I called around, looking for a spot for Janie. Mrs.—" She broke off, unable to give away an employee's name. "Someone here told me you had openings."

He pushed his glasses up his Ichabod Crane nose. "We're supposed to receive funds," he said. "But they don't reach us. Look in the pockets of your own bosses, or at the city council. That money never hits a public account, but the men and women who are supposed to help your friend are getting richer all the time. Check your own house before you accuse me of slacking."

Before she could catch her breath, he disappeared inside the cheap door that didn't even slam with impressive force. No one wasted money on the vinyl-furnished waiting room.

Janie rose from her green sofa. "No room at the inn?" She seemed pleased.

Could Thomas be right? Abby flattened her hand against her belly. Once the baby came, she didn't see inviting Janie to stay overnight no matter how desperate the other woman might be.

If she wasn't sure Thomas was healthy enough to

be a father, she certainly couldn't risk her baby with unstable friends, no matter how much she cared about Janie.

She met the other woman halfway across the waiting room. "We can't stay," she said.

Janie's smile broke her heart. So hopeful and yet wounded. She'd promised several times in the car that this time was different. She wanted to stop drinking. Find a real life.

"You're right. No room after all." Abby didn't share Dr. Gatehouse's theory. "The nurse I spoke to must have been wrong."

"Where do we go now?"

"Reverend Michael's out." She'd called him on the way over, but he'd said Janie had caused too much chaos the last time she'd stayed. "Let me start through my list again as we drive back."

They walked, side by side, down the walkway. In her car, the odor of alcohol that clung to Janie made Abby nauseous. She felt guilty and rude.

She let down her window an inch or so and then started dialing. After several fruitless inquiries, she began to feel desperate. Shelters waited until afternoon to start admitting people. No one wanted Janie this early in the day.

"I could stay with you," Janie suggested, her voice tentative.

Abby leaned her head toward the window, trying to be inconspicuous as she drank in fresh air. "I can't."

"Because of your boyfriend?"

All of Thomas's cautions repeated in her mind. "My what?"

"You don't want him to know you're with me."

"What do you mean?"

"You're ashamed of me. You don't want that man to know about me."

Imagine Thomas being right. "He's staying in my guest room. I don't have space for anyone else," she said. "And you need to clean up and find your own place, Janie."

"You never said that before. What changed you?"

Her baby. Thomas's and her baby. She'd risk her child's well-being for no one. "I've always wanted you to sober up."

"But you never acted like you didn't want to be around me."

Janie, in her quiet dignity, left hints of the woman she'd been before her life had imploded.

"I'll always be your friend. You can count on me."

"I don't need friends."

Abby was almost relieved at her hard-done-by tone. Resentment, she could handle. Janie, with a broken heart—it just hurt too much. They'd been friends for a long time, and Abby still hoped she'd find a better life.

They were almost downtown again before she found a place that would take Janie. When she hung up, her friend looked faintly relieved.

"I'll be good tonight," Janie said.

"Let's try to find another treatment center tomorrow. If I look for one, will you go and make a real effort?"

"Yes."

"It won't work unless you want to change." Abby glanced at her.

"I want to." Janie wrinkled her mouth. "I don't want to lose you to a bottle."

"It's not about me. Living on the streets isn't safe." She breathed deep, her stomach still rolling. "Honestly, I worry I'll go in to work one day and hear you've died."

"I won't," Janie said. "Although maybe we'd all be better off...."

"No." Tensing, Abby hit the brakes and the car jerked. Janie tilted forward and then back, but she smiled as if she heard ideas in voices that Abby couldn't discern. "You have to try, Janie. You're getting worse."

"I'll take care." Janie patted her own legs, a woman making a decision. "Let's get through today. I'll make my life right."

Abby walked Janie into the shelter. Once she began to settle her coat and things around her bed for the night, Abby returned to the office to ask the young woman on duty to keep an extra vigilant eye on her. Tomorrow, first thing, she'd find a better and more permanent place for her friend.

Back in the car, she picked up her phone and dialed Catherine's office to report what Dr. Gatehouse had told her. Catherine's voice mail kicked in.

Abby hesitated as she waited through Catherine's message. After warning her friend about Harv Stuckey's story, she didn't want to seem obsessed in front of her boss.

But how many people were going without treatment? "Catherine, Abby again. I spoke to Dr. Gatehouse at the Friendship Center today. I wanted to enter a woman in their alcohol program, but he tells me the funds for the indigent have gone dry." She explained the rest and hung up.

The facts sounded sinister, but Catherine would know who to send looking for waylaid funds.

LIAM CALLED TO CANCEL their session again. Thomas didn't complain. He'd discovered a few important changes on his own, and he'd just as soon Liam didn't see the threats on Abby's walls. They were Abby's story to tell her ex-husband.

He dressed for his run and went out, checking the sides of the house first to make sure no one was lurking in the shrubbery. Everything looked empty.

He ran with more energy than usual and considered adding distance to his circuit, but those notes on Abby's garage bothered him. She shouldn't have to face them just because she was doing her job. He turned back to start cleaning them before she came home.

The streets and her yard were still quiet, but he stuck to his habit of checking for intruders. Abby called him paranoid. That didn't worry him as much as the idea that someone might come after her.

He showered quickly and found cleaning supplies, a pail of hot water and mild, liquid soap and the fluffy sponge Abby used to clean her car. He managed to erase all but a shadow of the painted words. He backed away from the wall to take a final, dissatisfied look. Her house was older, the siding real wood instead of vinyl.

The siding looked freshly painted and he'd seen some paint in the garage. He swept and put down a drop cloth and then sorted through the paint, searching for the right green. A god-awful purple can made him laugh out loud. In Abby's cozy home?

Suddenly, a shadow passed in front of the garage window in front of him. He dropped his head, ducking instinctively. Someone had stolen into the backyard.

Meter reader? He doubted it. Someone who'd already grown tired of leaving bland messages?

Thomas set the paint on the floor and eased to the next window. Nothing stirred. Abby kept her gates too well-oiled. A squeak would have been useful. He assumed the intruder had already made his way into the backyard.

He eased back into the house and stole to the kitchen. His pulse seemed to ricochet between his ears. Pictures flashed in his head, blinding him. The corporal who'd reached for one of the kids in that small, hot room. His hand had exploded in front of Thomas's face.

That was the moment he'd known things were going bad.

He groaned and rubbed his eyes. Then he crouched to get to the kitchen door without showing himself in the windows.

Maybe this clown was still playing games, but what if he'd come tonight to make good on his threats? Thomas had to stop him before he got to Abby.

Sticking by the counters that ringed the room, Thomas edged to the knife block. He tested a couple of knives before he found one whose weight he liked.

Only the bad guy got hurt today.

A figure started up the porch steps, face hidden in the depths of a too-big hooded sweatshirt. Thomas resisted a reckless urge to fly through the door. Wait. Choose the right moment.

The hood went back. Janie.

Janie, alone. What about Abby?

He pictured her parking, coming up the walk alone, not knowing her "friend" had broken into the house to wait for her.

No freakin' way.

He hit the floor and slid to the porch door, scan-

ning the glass fronts in the appliances across the
kitchen for any hint of movement.

Come on in.

Think. How could this woman get back before
Abby?

The doorknob squeaked. Once, twice. And then
she rattled it so hard the door shook against his back.

Janie was angry.

She didn't have Abby. Modify the plan. To hell
with Janie on the porch. He had to reach Abby in
front before Janie gave up in back.

Thomas took to the shelter of the cabinets again.
It wasn't foolproof. When he reached the hall, he'd
be in plain sight if Janie stopped beating on the door
to look.

He had no choice. Abby'd be back any second.

He was on his feet the moment he hit the shadows in the hall. Pounding for the front door, he decided against hitting the alarm's panic buttons.

He could use a cop, but why warn Janie?

She might be armed. Abby had left her gun in the
safe. She'd be carrying nothing.

Thomas drummed out the alarm code and turned
to the front door. The kitchen went silent. He
snapped open the door's dead bolt and scanned the
yard.

At the bottom of the walkway, Abby looked toward
Janie rounding the side yard. Thomas could only see
Janie's hood, but whatever Abby saw made her run.

At unbelievable speed, Janie closed in on her prey.

Abby spied him. "Gun," she said.

He lifted the knife. At the same time, Janie reached Abby and the two women struggled up the porch steps. Janie leveled the gun at Abby's head and Abby stopped.

Rage filmed Thomas's sight. He concentrated on Janie's shaking trigger finger, tested the knife in his hand.

He drew it back.

"No." Abby's voice cut through the haze. "She's sick. You can't kill an innocent woman."

"Abby." Saying her name hurt his throat. "Are you crazy?"

"Move and she dies," Janie said. "I'd rather kill her than leave her to you."

If her finger tightened at all, he'd throw.

"Release her."

"You're the crazy one." Janie laughed, pure happiness in her voice. "I found my baby."

"Abby?" She had to let him protect her.

"No. Can't you hear how disturbed she is?"

Janie laughed again.

Feelings he'd hidden for the past six years broke through the junk in his head. "I love you, Abby." He never shifted his gaze from Janie's hand. "You're not going to die."

"What?" Abby's voice was tight. Janie's grip kept her head canted to the left.

"Don't listen to him." Janie pushed her toward the door. "You—get out of the way. I'll take care of her."

Thomas stared harder. Didn't move. "Take care of her, Janie? Nothing's wrong with Abby."

"I won't lose her again."

Her voice rose. Thomas backed up. Inside, he could use the walls against her. He'd toss Abby behind the nearest piece of furniture.

"Janie, I'm not your daughter." Horror filled Abby's voice at last.

He wanted to kill Janie for making Abby that afraid.

"I lost you once because you had that other baby, but this time your father isn't here so I'll handle it. You can't leave me. We'll go together."

"Go?" Abby asked. "Where?"

"You know—leave it all, but together."

Damn it, he'd waited too long again. His hand vibrated with rage.

"Abby, duck," he said. The baby stuff made no sense, but Janie meant to kill herself and Abby. He'd seen too much suicide to miss the signs.

"Don't. I can do this." She shifted, trying to see the other woman, but Janie slid her hand to Abby's neck and pulled her back.

Thomas slowly lifted his hand, grateful for a second chance while Janie was distracted. Light glittered on the blade. It should have been blood.

"Janie," he said, "look at me. Watch me because I'm going to kill you the second you move."

"I can't let her have your baby. Her dad won't like it, and I can't let her keep leaving because of men and babies."

Thomas's knees buckled. "My baby? Abby, is this real?"

"Janie, you don't want to hurt the baby."

"I have to stop you, honey." She burrowed the gun into Abby's temple.

Thomas threw the knife. It took the hood of her sweatshirt into the wall and jerked her arm away. Abby snatched the gun. At the same time, Janie yanked the knife out of the wall. Thomas didn't know he'd moved, but he was standing in front of them both.

"Don't, Thomas." Abby trained the gun on her friend. "Janie, drop the knife."

"Oh, for God's sake." Thomas took the knife, and just managed to keep himself from breaking Janie's arm. "Abby, dial 911."

As Janie wept, Abby hesitated. "Don't hurt her. She can't help it."

"I chose not to kill her. But she's not coming near you again. Just call."

She ran into the living room, scrambling for the portable phone she could hardly ever find. At the same moment, Herb strolled into Thomas's peripheral vision. Janie continued to cry, the volume rising.

"Grab the cat, Abby."

Abby scooped him up, patted him on the head, to Thomas's annoyance, and opened the closet door. "Sorry, Herb, but we don't need you causing trouble." She set him among the shoes and finally dialed the police. When she hung up she put the phone on the floor.

"Let me help her, Thomas."

"She plays you, Abby. She'll be fine till some other cops get here."

She said nothing. He waited for her to explain about the baby. She didn't.

"Thank you for not hurting her. I would have felt responsible."

"What if she'd hurt you?" He saw the shot Janie had never fired, as if she had. He could imagine Abby's head rocking to the side. He shook his own head. Thoughts like that would take him off his guard. "What baby, Abby?"

"She must have gone through my garbage and found the test. Can we talk about it later?"

"We don't have to." Her plan was clear. They'd made a baby, but he'd only donated sperm.

"I want this baby. That's why I went to the hospital the other night. After the fight I thought something was wrong."

Angry and afraid, he wanted to hate her. "Well?" He couldn't let himself say more.

"They did an ultrasound. I'm still pregnant. They'll do another one next week, but I know I'm fine."

"What a relief." He sounded bitter because he was.

Sirens wailed, and Janie cut the crying at last. She looked up, and Thomas barely stopped himself from putting her on the ground. His instincts were rusty, wrong, but back.

"You'll come with me, Abby?" Janie begged, her face wet with tears.

"No." Abby said it with love that broke Thomas's heart. She knew how to love. She loved strangers. "You and I can't hang around together anymore, Janie. I'll check on your progress, but I seem to be bad for you to know."

"I'll be good. I won't try to make you stop having babies anymore."

Abby shuddered. "When you're sober, we'll talk."

She'd left out sane. A patrol car stopped outside. Thomas took Janie's arm. "Let's go."

The police took their statements. Thomas held his temper, moving out of the way after the patrolmen finished with him.

He'd felt like this the day his men had died. He had rights, but all he could think was that Abby had walked away before. Last night at her parents' she'd asked him when he'd be finished with Liam. She'd wanted him out of Houston before he found out about his child.

He waited on the fringes while the patrolmen questioned Abby and Janie. When the younger man finally helped Janie into the car, Abby walked with them. "Please be careful with her."

Thomas gave up in disgust. He pivoted toward the house and proceeded upstairs to pack.

"ABBY, SHE WANTED TO KILL YOU. I don't think you can cure her with kindness." The older patrolman obviously shared Thomas's opinion of her gullibility as he got in his car and drove away with Janie.

Abby didn't watch. "This is where I start being smart." She turned back to the house, but Thomas had disappeared. He'd be packing.

She went inside and closed the door. Then she set the alarm and checked it. She ran up the stairs, prepared to knock down Thomas's door.

He'd left it open, relieving her of the need for dramatics. She lost her nerve, but forced herself to walk in. He'd already stripped the bed and was ramming his things into his bag.

"Let me explain," she said.

"You can't." He didn't bother to look at her. "You think I'm damaged. You think I'm unstable. You think I'm not fit to be a father."

"The moment I realized Janie might be on the verge of killing me I understood what my mother's been telling me all along. You had the right to know about your own baby, and I should have been the one to tell you." She could never apologize enough, never explain how deeply she regretted not telling him. She'd never understand if she were the one who'd been—betrayed. But Thomas looked at her, his whole body tensed, furious, accusing her. She'd done something else wrong.

"You told your parents?"

"That makes it worse?"

"You told them but you couldn't tell me?"

She knotted her hand in the hem of her shirt. "That night in the hospital, I was so afraid, and no one else knew. I needed someone." His shattered expression stopped her. "I guess telling Mom and Dad does make it worse, but Thomas, I thought I was losing the baby."

"You should have called the baby's father."

"You didn't know I wasn't using birth control. You didn't ask for the responsibility, and I still don't believe you should have to make a decision when you're not—"

"Stable?" He slapped another shirt into his bag.

"Yourself," she said. "I knew you were ill. I've lived with my mother's illness all my life. My parents decided not to have more children because they realized early on I wasn't having a childhood." She freed her hands and spread them. "Please, I tried to do the right thing."

"For you." He stopped packing to come to her. "Because you were scared of my problems. I decide what's best for me. I don't need your lousy decisions. And as for my baby, no matter what happens between us, you're not raising my child alone."

"Lousy decisions? You mean when I left North Carolina?"

"I should have come after you then, but even I didn't believe I was giving you enough."

She cut in. "How would you give more to a child? How's a baby supposed to understand a father flying into danger *all* the time?"

He zeroed in with a killer's smile. "Leaving without a fight isn't the same as making a decision. Neither is lying to yourself. You'd lie down on railroad tracks for a friend like Janie because it's all one-sided. She's not capable of loving you. I am. But I expect you to love me back, not to take care of me."

"You're not making sense." She lied. He knew her. Giving was easier than taking. Taking put her in danger. She'd taken his love once. "You almost destroyed me."

"That's the way it is when two extremely different people love each other. You have to fight to stay together. You think you love, Abby, but you run scared."

"Maybe I did, but I'm not now. Stay, and I'll show you." Show him what? That she wanted him for all time? That she wasn't afraid? What a laugh. If she could be that kind of actress, she'd have toughed it out before and pretended she was happy. She'd loved him that much.

Maybe she still did.

"Stay." She looked straight into his cold blue eyes.

"You're lying."

"No."

"Everything changed for you in that split second with Janie? Right. I won't stay and let you lie to me or yourself." He picked up his bag with all his stuff hanging over its zippered edges. "And I won't give up my child. Someone from base Legal will be in touch with you about custody."

Stunned, she listened to his footsteps, taking him away from her. The wounded Thomas was gone. Him, she could have talked to. He would have tried to understand. This Thomas, his own man again, was proud to keep her at more than arm's length.

He didn't need her.

CHAPTER FOURTEEN

"LIAM?" THOMAS STARED through the hotel window at the clear night sky, warmer than his heart this evening. "Thomas here."

"Where are you?"

"I don't remember the name of the hotel." And he didn't bother to look.

"Something's happened."

"Abby's okay, but her friend Janie's been stalking her for the past few weeks, and she finally lost control today. She tried to break into the house and we had to call the police." Let Abby tell the rest if she wanted him to know. "I think your job is done, Liam."

Abby's ex waited, but this time Thomas felt no need to explain.

"What happened with Janie?" Liam's anxious voice reminded Thomas he wasn't the only one who'd loved Abby to no avail. "She tried to hurt you both?"

"She threatened us, but I finally grasped what you tried to make me understand. I'm fallible, but I forget when I go into battle. It's enough to keep doing the job."

"You stopped Janie?"

"Abby and I stopped her together. Maybe the only time we've ever worked as a team."

"You're going home?"

He anticipated his house in the small town outside Ft. Bragg about as much as he would an empty tent back in the desert. "That's why I called."

"And Abby?"

"What about her?"

"Where's she going?"

"Not with me."

"I wasn't asking that."

"You were, but I don't blame you." Maybe she'd turn to Liam again. She'd thought she loved him enough to marry him before. "Thank you for helping me. I'll expect your bill. Abby has the address."

"You'll call her before you leave?"

Anger burned, a fire in the back of his throat. "I've always known I'm particularly fallible when I'm mad, and I've never been this hot about anything before." He shouldn't have dropped such a large hint, but Abby couldn't hide the baby forever, and maybe it would be a good thing if Liam talked to her.

"Don't make this mistake again," Liam said. "Going without settling the carnage between you two just keeps the argument open."

"I'm making the only choice I have."

"MOM, NOT THE TEDDIES." Abby snatched them out of her suitcase and tossed them at the dresser. "I'll take pajamas. North Carolina will be colder, and the way Thomas felt when he left, I'll need more than a teddy to win him back."

"You told him and he still left?"

"You know he did."

"I didn't expect that." Elaine scooped up the blackest, most diaphanous teddy. "Just take this one. Call it your weapon of last resort."

Abby hugged her and scooped the clutter of toiletries off her bathroom counter into her bag. "I'm sorry the place is such a mess."

"If my child's father abandoned me and didn't even call for a week, tidying up wouldn't be my first priority."

In the old days a tidy environment had kept her mother calm. "What would be?"

"Making sure he didn't want me."

Abby pushed the teddy to the bottom. "I'm trying to make sure he does." Herb emerged from the bed skirt, and they both jumped. "He's mourned Thomas, too."

"I guess you have to bring him back for the whole family. Besides, I've heard pregnant women should avoid cat litter. You need someone to clean that for you."

And that was all her baby was good for? "I thought you liked Thomas now."

"I'll try to because you still love him." Elaine locked her hands beneath Herb's belly and lifted him. "Don't worry about a thing here. We'll look after this big boy. You find out if Thomas loves you, and then don't run away from any more sick people."

"It wasn't just because of you." Abby stroked her cat's head. "I'm frightened of losing love. I always knew you loved me."

"But I kept going to my own secret place, and I tried to hide it from you and your father. You grew up, but you cope as if you were still the little girl who witnessed her mother's worst years. Tell Thomas."

"You have all the answers except the one I need."

Her mom tossed in a hairbrush and a pair of sneakers. "What's that?"

"Faith in myself." Abby rubbed her temple. "I think I can handle his job. I'd rather be with him than worry about losing him. I'll try with all my heart because I can't live without him anymore." She heard the flaw in her own argument. "But what if I can't live up to my promises when he's continually in danger? What about our baby then?"

"We choose to live despite the worst things that can happen. You also choose to love. Your child will be safe because you'll know how to teach him or her that people just endure the bad times and survive. We enjoy the good, and if we're smart, we're grateful for both." Elaine looked at the nightstand clock. "Didn't you say you were lunching with friends?"

"Oh, yeah. Lucy and Risa." Abby scanned the room, appalled at all she was leaving undone. And what would she do if he took her back? She still had a job. A home with a mortgage. "Mom, what if he sends me away?"

"I doubt it would be final." Elaine shooed her toward the door. "You're going to be late for your friends."

"Why are you suddenly so sure?"

"Because I've kept my family all these years. We've loved each other enough to stay together when it would have been easier for your father to divorce me or you to move to Timbuktu and find a nice safe police job chasing smugglers—or whatever you chase in Timbuktu."

Abby kissed her mom's cheek. "You're braver than I am."

"Now that would surprise me." Elaine reached for her daughter, but stumbled over Herb, performing his feed-me dance. She scooped him up again, and he overflowed her arms. "You go, and I'll finish here."

Abby flung an arm around her mom and kissed her on the cheek. "Thanks." She ran down and grabbed her purse on her way to the door, but then she skidded back to the stairs. "Mom? You know the alarm for when you leave?" She wouldn't soon forget the feeling of Janie's gun at her head.

"I wrote it on my hand."

Abby tried not to laugh. "That works." She'd put it on paper before she left for North Carolina, in case her parents had to come in while she was gone.

She drove to the coffee shop where Risa and Lucy had agreed to meet her. She found them at the same table Risa had taken before.

Risa, her dark hair in a ponytail, her lovely face animated, stopped, midconversation. "Abby, you look a little green around the gills."

"I guess the word will get out. I'm a little pregnant."

Lucy turned with a serious smile that emphasized her startling, girl-next-door beauty. Dark auburn hair brushed her shoulders as she rose for a hug.

"I'm so glad to see you."

"Me, too. I'm sorry the others couldn't come." Abby took the third chair. "But I'm glad you guys did."

Risa touched her hands. "You're going after Thomas again? Maybe he should come this way."

"He just left." Abby should have felt odd admitting this to friends who'd been estranged for months. But, together again, it felt like the old days. "I didn't tell him about the baby."

"Oh," Risa said. "That doesn't seem like you."

"I wasn't my finer self with this decision." She smoothed her own ponytail. "I have to go back anyway, to see if I can stand his life again before I beg him to forgive me."

"The agonies of love," Lucy said with a laugh.

Abby nodded. "I didn't think Thomas could handle a baby."

"Nothing much could make a man feel less manly." As usual, Risa saw straight to the point.

Abby could persuade Thomas she knew he was a man anytime. Persuading him she trusted him? That seemed to be more difficult. She changed the subject. "How's Grady?"

"Perfect."

"I didn't know perfect existed."

"You don't know Grady." Risa sounded smug, but who wouldn't?

Abby turned to Lucy, who was smirking at their friend. "And this Jackson I hear of?"

"He's working on the ranch. He'll be back in a few days."

"You're both so happy. Did you ever worry it might not work out?"

Lucy nodded, as did Risa, but Lucy spoke. "You have to be willing to leap into love despite the risk. You have to make it fit with the rest of your life. Otherwise, maybe you don't love enough."

"Do you mind if I say that to Thomas if he tries to throw me out?"

"He doesn't know you're coming?" Risa asked.

"No."

"What if he's not there?"

"I'm turning the logistics over to fate." She smiled at their doubtful expressions. "It's no leap if you don't take risks. He might leave if I tell him I'm coming, and what he needs to know is that I did come. If he's gone, I'll leave a message."

"What if he asks you to marry him again?" Lucy

covered her coffee cup as their server came to take Abby's order.

"No," Abby said, mindful of the caffeine. "I'd like lemonade."

"You'd move there again?" Risa asked.

"I'm on leave from the department. I've been steeling myself to ask you to be my references." Abby grinned. "Thomas has three more years before he retires, and I thought I could lobby the local police department for a CIT team if he relents."

"He'll relent." Risa's confidence eased the anxiety gnawing at the pit of Abby's stomach. "Where'd he go when he was in trouble? Straight to you. He's upset, but he'll forgive you."

"I hope you're right."

"I just want you to have friends around you if something goes wrong."

"We're always going to be friends after this," Lucy said. "And we'll know how to find each other."

Abby frowned. "We find each other, but we're not all okay together. Or we'd all be here."

Risa and Lucy shared her worried glance. Risa lifted her coffee cup. "If you wear Thomas down, we'll start next on our other friends."

THAT NIGHT, TUCKED UP in her warm, safe bed, she called Harv. She'd tried him three times before. In between, she'd dialed Janie's public defender, who was trying to work a plea that got her into a good facility.

Startling Abby, Harv finally answered his phone. His slurred response was barely intelligible. "How are you?" An inane question, but how else could she ask if he was still alive, if he'd stopped taking chances?

"I'm drunk. Normally I try to hide it, but whattha-hell. I might have news for you soon."

Her instincts went on alert. "What kind of news?"

"Ne'er mind. I'll call ya." And he hung up.

He wouldn't answer when she dialed him back. She tried twice more before she gave up and dialed Catherine. She was home, thank goodness.

"Hi, it's Abby."

"Abby?" She clearly didn't want to talk.

"I'm taking some time off, and I wondered if you'd check in on Harv occasionally. He's the guy who—"

"I haven't forgotten."

"Are you all right?" Abby sat up straighter, pulling the bedclothes tight around her waist. "Have you discovered something about Jordan?"

"No. Don't worry about it. Have a good time and be assured I'll check on Harv."

"Okay."

"And, Abby?"

"Yes?"

"Why don't you call me when you come back to work?"

Her tone asked for understanding. Abby didn't

have to look for it. "We'll meet for a drink." Whether she came back to work or not, she was leaving family and beloved friends here. She'd be back.

"I'd like that," Catherine said. "It's been too long since we've shared a drink."

They said goodbye, and Abby smiled in anticipation of meeting another of her old friends for a drink, rather than business. Too bad she'd be knocking back the lemonade. She must be full to the eyes of lemonade.

"I'M SORRY. I LOVE YOU." She tried again. "I love you. I'm sorry." Which would be more important to Thomas? Neither had mattered in Houston.

Practicing as she followed the gray-black road between tall Southern pines hardly eased her nervousness. This was too important to work up an impressive presentation.

She felt around in her own mind for the right words, but her heart had kept its secrets too long. She hardly trusted herself. How could she convince Thomas she really wanted to try again?

By the time she turned into the woods that led to his house, her heart was hammering, and a clutter of memories filled her mind. Her first hopeful days here with Thomas. Driving through tears in the other direction the day she'd left.

Knowing she should have faced him.

At least she was doing that right this time. If only

he found sending her away more difficult than walking out.

The foliage that lined the road to his house had grown taller. Though spiny with winter's cold, it was familiar and oddly strange, all at the same time. She'd never expected to see it again.

She almost missed his driveway. He'd installed lamps to light the way, and he'd planted box hedges to shield himself from the road.

She turned in, slowing, as she saw Thomas, splitting logs for the fireplace. She'd always teased him about his rustic woodpile, situated beside the kitchen door. Practical, because he needed the firewood, he still managed to make it fit with the small, dark brick house he'd restored in Spartan style.

But did he see her head each time he swung that ax with so much enthusiasm?

He only heard her as she stopped in front of the one-car garage that had never had room for her. He turned, but looked guarded. Not happy.

Jumping nerves made her feel sick as she climbed out of the car. Thomas, in jeans and a thermal shirt, wiped his sleeve across his forehead.

Longing struck her, need as palpable as the blood that ran in her veins, the life that grew inside her. She'd flown from Houston on the strength of a belief that wasn't real. Thomas might not love her. She might be wrong about all she believed they could share.

She shut the door and marched around the car. Fear? Oh, she was terrified. But she loved Thomas, and she had to tell him, had to offer him a life with her and their child if he could love her, too.

He stared at her, any emotion he had hidden.

"I ran *to* you, instead of away," she said.

He obviously didn't appreciate her glib attempt at courage. "This time," he said. "I've noticed the planes go both ways."

"I'd hoped you'd forgive and forget as soon as you saw me."

"Did you do either when I showed up on your doorstep?"

"No." Her breath wisped in the freezing air. "Not at first, but I took a chance on you."

Something flickered in his eyes. Warmth, surprise, awareness?

"Can't you take a chance on me, too?" She couldn't control her softening tone. She needed him so much, and she'd never made herself vulnerable to anyone. Not even to him, really.

"Why?"

"I have to convince you?" Fear made her want to dump him and run, but she'd been that foolish before. "I wouldn't have left if I'd believed you wanted me more than your job. I wanted to come first."

"Me, too," he said. "What's the answer?"

"We have to keep trying even when we hate each other."

He shook his head. Exhaustion ruddied his face like the hot sun. "I don't want you to hate me."

"You love your job—I want you to be safe. You wish I'd be more careful—I can't help going too far when people need me. Neither one of us knows how to give in. We're going to hate each other." She used her own sleeve to wipe his forehead. He jumped, caught her arm, but didn't let go. She dared a little more. "I love you." She fastened her gaze to his fingers wrapped in her shirt. An odd symbol of hope. "And I'm focused on this baby we made."

He tried to release her, but she turned her hand and held on to his wrist.

"You came because of the baby?" he asked.

"I came because I love you," she said again. "I came to fight. If we want each other, we can make a family."

"What about our old problems, Abby? They haven't changed." His voice throbbed.

Her hope grew a little stronger. She inspected the beard already growing, his long hair, still uncut. "You're about to leave?"

"Soon." She glimpsed shadows of old pain in the lines of his face.

"I'll wait for you here if you want to come home to me."

"What's changed, Abby? I'm safe for you now?"

"Safe may be a temporary state no one gets to enjoy for long. My mom said you had a right to know, even if you never recovered from what happened to you. I don't know if we recover from post-traumatic stress. Maybe that's why I don't want to be abandoned—for illness or a compulsion to carry out duty."

"I never put my duty before you," he said. "Maybe I couldn't let you fill my heart before because I had to keep my mind free for the job." He stopped, his eyes narrowed. "Why are you smiling?"

"I never expected you to talk about full hearts." He'd tried too hard to look invincible.

Finally, his eyes grew tender, in the old, rare way. "You do fill mine, Abby, but I'm not sure that's enough. I have to go back to work."

"I know."

"And I could die."

"But what will my life be like if I don't spend it with you?" Heat suffused her whole body. "That sounds selfish, but I want to live with you. I want our child to know his father."

"You already know it's a boy?"

"Or *her* father."

"Did you have that second ultrasound?"

She grinned with happiness too fierce to contain. "I'm fine, and they gave me a picture, but the baby looks a little beanlike."

"What changed your mind, Abby?" He wasn't ready to give in.

"Janie and her gun. I threw away six years that

might have been happy. I cheated you of the news of your own child."

He nodded, but with mistrust.

Abby let him go. He had to make the next move. "I'll take the chance that everything could go completely wrong and we'll hate each other till our dying breaths. But we might learn to live together, despite the fact that we don't always think alike, and we might love each other so much we'll be good parents. We might even make each other happy."

"And you won't leave again?"

"You left this time."

"You won't lie to protect me when I'm lost in the job I have to do?"

"I won't lie." She pushed her hands down her sides. Giving up control was like jumping into the wind. "Period." She lifted her chin, backsliding just a little. "But you'll try not to get killed?"

He narrowed his eyes, and the skin tightened across his cheekbones. He stared at her so long she couldn't tell what he was thinking. Finally, a smile relaxed his mouth.

"I might have tried anyway, but I'll make an extra effort for you."

She loved his teasing tone, but silence fell between them. She didn't know how to break it. She'd fought her attraction to him for so long. Ridiculous, considering she carried his child.

"I love you, Thomas."

"Why don't we go inside and figure out what comes next?"

"In a sec." She looped an arm around his neck and pulled his face down to hers. He kept his eyes open, and she saw love. As fierce and sure and full of longing as she'd ever felt. "I do love you. Can't you say it, too?"

"I thought I had." He looked as if he hurt. "It's all I hear in my head."

She touched her lips to his. Wonder made her tentative until he wrapped her in his arms, groaning as if he'd believed they'd never touch again. With his mouth he destroyed her last safe boundary, taking revenge, demanding penance, giving of himself.

Her head swam and her knees trembled when she found her feet again. She was cold in the wind without Thomas's body swathing her.

"Well?" he asked, impatient, pulling her toward his house.

"I can always bring my things out of the car tomorrow."

She stumbled up the rough-hewn steps, already in his arms again, already risking everything.

EPILOGUE

WARM HANDS SLID beneath Abby's sweatshirt as she huddled into the bedclothes. The teddy her mom had thought so important was still deep in the bottom of Abby's bag. She couldn't seem to keep warm in North Carolina unless Thomas spooned up behind her in bed as he did this early March morning.

She studied their clothes, strewn around his bedroom. They'd shared the room for more than a week, but she never seemed to actually unpack. If he followed her in, more urgent matters always distracted them.

"Are you going to marry me, Abby? Before our baby comes?"

She glanced at the ultrasound print he'd taped to the mirror on top of his bureau. He'd circled the baby with a red heart.

"I'll marry you whenever you want," she said.

"Should we do it in Houston?"

She rolled over, and her heart half broke at the raw love in his eyes. "Mom and Dad would like that," she said. "And I wouldn't mind a ceremony at home."

"When?" He kissed one of her eyes and then the other. "Before I leave next Thursday? We could get a quick flight."

Fear grabbed at Abby, but she resisted it. If he could face going back into a life that had shown him hell, she could face her images of it.

"I know you'll come home again," she said, her tone thick, her eyes wide-open to let him see she was honest. "Let's wait until you have time off after the trip."

Beneath her sweatshirt, his hand found her breast. He caught her mouth with passion as unbridled as they'd found it that night in her house. Still, the ringing phone cut through the heat between them.

They both lived their work lives by the demands of a ringing phone, and they both had responsibilities outside the cocoon of love they'd finally made secure.

"Not this time," Thomas said against her mouth.

Laughing, she turned her face into his throat, drinking in his scent. "You surprise me."

"Don't answer the phone, and I'll surprise you some more."

His deft hands had started a race her body needed to finish, but she couldn't forget how vulnerable her mother remained, uncertain she could count on Abby's and Thomas's reassurance that they were together.

"Wait—let me just make sure it's not Mom."

"Hurry."

While he slid his hand restlessly down her belly, she grabbed the phone off the nightstand and read the caller ID. "Holy…" She couldn't believe the name that flashed up, and she punched the Talk button before she thought. "Mei Lu, you called! Excuse me while I persuade the man of my dreams I need some time to talk to an old friend."

Thomas, disagreeing, slid down her body. As his lips closed on her navel, she hoped Mei Lu survived her startled cry of laughter.

Laughter born of the truest love couldn't hurt anyone.

*Please turn the page to read an excerpt from
the next book in the* WOMEN IN BLUE
series from Superromance.
SHE WALKS THE LINE
*by Roz Denny Fox is available in February
wherever Harlequin books are sold.*

CHAPTER ONE

MEI LU LING SHRUGGED into her shoulder holster and slid it into place. She took a moment to reflect on last Friday's ceremony, which allowed her to walk into Houston PD headquarters a full-fledged lieutenant. Only two of her four best friends from the academy, a twenty-six week class that now seemed a distant memory, had attended her ceremony, even though Mei had invited them all.

She'd noticed Crista Santiago at the back of the room, and Risa Taylor had popped in long enough to see Catherine Tanner, the chief, do the honors. Mei was happy her new department captain had had a court commitment, and that Catherine had volunteered to replace him. It also pleased her that two of her friends had been able to slip away from their duties. Especially Risa, considering everything she'd undergone not so long ago at the hands of the internal review board. Risa and Crista were the only members of their once close-knit group who knew what it was like to struggle up the department ladder without family support. And none of Mei's family would have put in an appearance if their lives depended on it.

But at thirty-one, after more than six years as a cop, Mei had no regrets. She was content with her life and career solving white-collar crime in the city where she'd been born and raised.

Still, it was well-known that women on the force had to take extra care to dot every *i* and cross every *t*. More so than a man working a similar case. Police departments had long been bastions for perpetuating good-old-boy philosophies. It helped that Mei and the four other women had entered the academy at a time when Catherine Tanner served as an instructor. She'd helped then avoid the pitfalls she'd had to navigate. Nevertheless, Mei was again reminded of Risa's recent problems with Internal Affairs. She'd been accused of shooting her partner, which had sparked a messy investigation that had affected their jobs. As a result, their trust in one another had shattered. Mei, Crista, Lucy Montalvo and Abby Carlton had temporarily stopped meeting for any reason. Heck, who was she kidding? The friends were still scattered. Risa's problem had left seemingly irreparable damage to their friendship. They'd all become a lot more wary about confiding in peers. As well, Risa's ordeal had left Mei Lu feeling extra worried about a summons of the type that crinkled in her pocket as she was shown into the chief's office by Annette Hayworth, Catherine's personal assistant.

Mei's qualms tripled when Catherine, lacking her normal smile, rose from her desk and shut the door before directing her to a chair. Lately, everyone had sensed an unusual tension in their chief. Since Catherine made such a point of closing the door, Mei assumed this call was personal and, therefore, serious.

"I called you here to discuss a new case that's come to my attention," Catherine said abruptly. She picked up a yellow pad and thumbed back two or three pages.

"Ah. Another pillar in our community suspected of corporate crime?" Mei finally smiled. A degree in Business Administration, plus having served three years in her father's Hong Kong office, gave her an advantage over others in her department.

"This case is unusual," Catherine continued. "It appears we have a ring of smugglers here. Asian artifacts," she said. "Rare pieces, I'm told."

Mei's stomach tightened. Her father, Michael Ling, and her brother, Stephen, bought and sold high-end Asian art. Ling Limited dealt in expensive, often one-of-a-kind, authentic Chinese works, many of them antique. Surely Catherine didn't suspect Mei's family of anything unethical?

"I received a call from a Brett Davis at Interpol. Cullen Archer, a patron in the Houston art world, is their local contact. Actually Archer is a notable insurance investigator. I'm told he's scrupulous and has a history of producing results for our foreign

counterparts when it comes to tracking stolen paint-
ings and such."

"I'm happy to serve any way I can," Mei said,
bowing her head. "But if Mr. Archer is so effective,
how can I possibly augment his work?"

"I'm assigning you for several reasons, not the
least of which is your dedication to the investigative
process. I trust you implicitly and this case is classi-
fied, Mei Lu. The missing pieces are from Beijing
museums. High-ranking officials stand to lose their
jobs if the items aren't located." Catherine tore off
a sheet of paper and wrote in bold, broad strokes.
"This is Mr. Archer's home address. He's expecting
you within the hour."

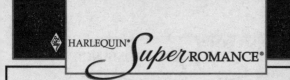

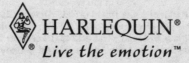

HARLEQUIN *Super*ROMANCE®

A six-book series from Harlequin Superromance

WOMEN *in* Blue

Six female cops battling crime and corruption on the streets of Houston. Together they can fight the blue wall of silence. But divided, will they fall?

Coming in February 2005, *She Walks the Line* by Roz Denny Fox (Harlequin Superromance #1254)

As a Chinese woman in the Houston Police Department, Mei Lu Ling is a minority twice over. She once worked for her father, a renowned art dealer specializing in Asian artifacts, so her new assignment—tracking art stolen from Chinese museums—is a logical one. But when she's required to work with Cullen Archer, an insurance investigator connected to Interpol, her reaction is more emotional than logical. Because she could easily fall in love with this man…and his adorable twins.

Coming in March 2005, *A Mother's Vow* by K. N. Casper (Harlequin Superromance #1260)

There is corruption in Police Chief Catherine Tanner's department. So when evidence turns up to indicate that her husband may not have died of natural causes, she has to go outside her own precinct to investigate. Ex-cop Jeff Rowan is the most logical person for her to turn to. Unfortunately, Jeff isn't inclined to help Catherine, considering she was the one who fired him.

Available wherever Harlequin books are sold.

Also in the series:
The Partner by Kay David (#1230, October 2004)
The Children's Cop by Sherry Lewis (#1237, November 2004)
The Witness by Linda Style (#1243, December 2004)
Her Little Secret by Anna Adams (#1248, January 2005)

www.eHarlequin.com   HSRWIB0105

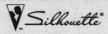

If you enjoyed what you just read,
then we've got an offer you can't resist!

Take 2 bestselling
love stories FREE!
Plus get a FREE surprise gift!

Clip this page and mail it to Harlequin Reader Service®

IN U.S.A.
3010 Walden Ave.
P.O. Box 1867
Buffalo, N.Y. 14240-1867

IN CANADA
P.O. Box 609
Fort Erie, Ontario
L2A 5X3

YES! Please send me 2 free Harlequin Superromance® novels and my free surprise gift. After receiving them, if I don't wish to receive anymore, I can return the shipping statement marked cancel. If I don't cancel, I will receive 6 brand-new novels every month, before they're available in stores. In the U.S.A., bill me at the bargain price of $4.69 plus 25¢ shipping and handling per book and applicable sales tax, if any*. In Canada, bill me at the bargain price of $5.24 plus 25¢ shipping and handling per book and applicable taxes**. That's the complete price, and a savings of at least 10% off the cover prices—what a great deal! I understand that accepting the 2 free books and gift places me under no obligation ever to buy any books. I can always return a shipment and cancel at any time. Even if I never buy another book from Harlequin, the 2 free books and gift are mine to keep forever.

135 HDN DZ7W
336 HDN DZ7X

Name	(PLEASE PRINT)	
Address	Apt.#	
City	State/Prov.	Zip/Postal Code

Not valid to current Harlequin Superromance® subscribers.

Want to try two free books from another series?
Call 1-800-873-8635 or visit www.morefreebooks.com.

* Terms and prices subject to change without notice. Sales tax applicable in N.Y.
** Canadian residents will be charged applicable provincial taxes and GST.
All orders subject to approval. Offer limited to one per household.
® are registered trademarks owned and used by the trademark owner and its licensee.

eHARLEQUIN.com

The Ultimate Destination for Women's Fiction

The eHarlequin.com online community is *the* place to share opinions, thoughts and feelings!

- Joining the community is easy, fun and **FREE!**

- Connect with **other romance fans** on our message boards.

- Meet your **favorite authors** without leaving home!

- **Share opinions** on books, movies, celebrities…and *more!*

Here's what our members say:

"I love the friendly and helpful atmosphere filled with support and humor."
—Texanna (eHarlequin.com member)

"Is this the place for me, or what? There is nothing I love more than 'talking' books, especially with fellow readers who are reading the same ones I am."
—Jo Ann (eHarlequin.com member)

**Join today by visiting
www.eHarlequin.com!**

INTCOMM04R

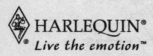

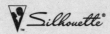

Lost & Found

Somebody's Daughter
by Rebecca Winters
Harlequin Superromance #1259

Twenty-six years ago, baby Kathryn was taken from the McFarland family. Now Kit Burke has discovered that she might have been that baby. Will her efforts to track down her real family lead Kit into their loving arms? Or will discovering that she is a McFarland mean disaster for her and the man she loves?

Available February 2005 wherever Harlequin books are sold.

Remember to look for these Rebecca Winters titles, available from Harlequin Romance:

To Catch a Groom (Harlequin Romance #3819)—on sale November 2004
To Win His Heart (Harlequin Romance #3827)—on sale January 2005
To Marry for Duty (Harlequin Romance #3835)—on sale March 2005

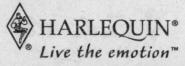

HARLEQUIN®
Live the emotion™